What

Henry Cartwright

The Mysteries of Stickleback Hollow

By C.S. Woolley

A Mightier Than the Sword UK Publication

©2018

What Became of Henry Cartwright

The Mysteries of Stickleback Hollow

By C. S. Woolley

A Mightier Than the Sword UK Publication

Paperback Edition

Paperback ISBN 978-0-9951470-5-8

Hardback ISBN 978-0-9951470-6-5

ePub ISBN 978-0-9951470-7-2

Kindle ISBN 978-0-9951470-8-9

iBooks ISBN 978-0-9951470-9-6

What became of Henry Cartwright
The place where the Birds don't follow

By C.B. Westley

A Mephad Than the Sword UK Production

Paperback edition

Paperback ISBN: 978-0-9954709-5-0
Hardback ISBN: 978-0-9954709-6-7
.pdf ISBN 978-0-9954709-7-4
Kindle ISBN 978-0-9954709-8-1
iBooks ISBN 978-0-9954709-9-8

Copyright Steve Westley 2018

Cover Design Steve Westley 2018

Cover Photo © Steve Raven 2016
(For more of Steve's work please visit . . .)

4

For Papa

For all your support, the grounding in history and the use of your British Empire books.

Thanks for taking the time to read *What Became of Henry Cartwright*, I hope you enjoy it, there is much more to come in the series if you do! This title is a little different to the rest of the series as the focus of the book is on the characters of the Brigadier, Countess Szonja, Chief Constable, Henry Cartwright and Miss Baker rather than on Lady Sarah, Mr Hunter and Constable Evans. But rest assured *The March of the Berry Pickers* will once again take readers back to Stickleback Hollow.

The Characters

Lady Sarah Montgomery Baird Watson-Wentworth

The heroine

Mr Alexander Hunter

A huntsman and groundskeeper of Grangeback

Doctor Jack Hales

The doctor in Stickleback Hollow

Lord Joshua St. Vincent

A young lord in the employ of Lady Carol-Ann

Mr Callum St. Vincent

A young gentleman in the employ of Lady Carol-Ann

Mr Harry Taylor

A gentleman from Staffordshire

Mr Henry Cartwright

Owner of Duffleton Hall

Mr Wilbraham Egerton

Son of Wilbraham & Elizabeth of Tatton Park

Lady Szonja, Countess of Huntingdon

Cousin of Elizabeth Egerton

Miss Angela Baker

A seamstress

Brigadier General George Webb-Kneelingroach

Guardian of Lady Sarah and owner of Grangeback

Superintendent Geoff Crump

Superintendent of Calcutta District Imperial Police

9

Samit

Childhood friend of Lady Sarah and manservant to Lady de Mandeville

John Smith

An Alias

Lady Carol-Ann Margaret de Mandeville, Duchess of Aumale and Montagu

Businesswoman in the East. Interests in Company Rule, the Orient and the continued strength of the Empire.

Commander Lin Tse-hsü

The Imperial High Commissioner of Canton

Captain Thomas Jonnes Smith

The Chief Constable of the Cheshire Constabulary

Chapter 1

and listen to the conversations the men held after dinner about the political situation they were trying to traverse.

Our world and views are shaped by our experiences. A sheltered life often leads to simplistic views, and too much exposure to the dangers of life creates a cynic. At least that is what Carol-Ann Margaret Cowdrey-Smithe had observed. She had spent her whole life surrounded by politics and business.

Lord Cowdrey-Smithe was a cold man. Though his family held a title, his father had lost most of their fortune gambling and drinking. Without a penny to his name and crippling debts, Lord Cowdrey-Smithe took his family to India as part of a diplomatic party.

Though his career in politics did not last long, there was plenty of other opportunities for the Cowdrey-Smithe family to make their mark on India.

Lady Carol-Ann was a young girl when her family went to India, and already there was diplomatic trouble between the British and China.

Though she was a woman and little more than a teenager, Lord Cowdrey-Smithe allowed his daughter to sit and listen to the conversations that the men held after dinner about the political situation they were trying to traverse.

"They deal with every foreign power as inferiors. They ignored our diplomatic credentials on our first visit; treated us like we were nothing more than barbarians," Lord Francis Napier said. Lord Napier was not part of the diplomatic mission to India or China. He had been a good friend to Lord Cowdrey-Smithe and had journeyed with his friend to see him settled in India before he returned to Britain.

"They cannot concede that another empire could be growing outside their borders, one that is superior to theirs in many ways," Lord Cowdrey-Smithe replied.

"We need to do something. The silver we are paying them for the silk and tea is crippling our interests," Mr Williams said. Mr Williams was one of the directors of the East India Company. He was not the only one of the Court of Directors in attendance.

Mr Francis Baring, the chairman of the Court of Directors of the East India Company, Mr William Bensley, Jacob Bosanquent and Mr John Smith Burges were also there.

"Their policy of refusing to trade with anyone in the normal manner is becoming increasingly frustrating. There is nothing they need to trade with us for. They have a self-sufficient economy," Mr Bensley shook his head with frustration.

"Their imports are half the value of their exports. There is no acknowledgement of diplomatic credentials or even the smallest about of courtesy extended to foreign dignitaries. We have to trade with the Chinese through the hong merchants, and they refuse to reduce the trade tariffs," Mr Burges growled as he threw back the contents of his port glass.

"If the French don't stop this preposterous war on the Crowned heads of Europe, we will need our silver to pay to defeat them. There must be something that we can export to China that can at least balance our trade with them," Mr Bosanquent mused as he gazed at the brandy in his glass.

"Excuse me, gentlemen, but I would have thought that the answer was obvious," Carol-Ann said from the sofa she was sat on. The seven men turned to look at the young lady with curiosity. They were used to her sitting in the room

13

without saying a word.

"Oh? What is it that mi'lady has in her mind?" Mr Baring asked as he stood and walked over to where Carol-Ann was sat.

"Mr Watson proposed an idea to the Company in regards to opium. We discussed the notion at great length before he made the proposal. The Company grows opium here in India. If the Company sends a ship filled with open to stand, say 13 miles offshore, and trades with smugglers for a year, you could increase the demand for opium in China very easily," Carol-Ann replied with a slight shrug.

"And if we only accept silver for the opium then we can balance our payments," Mr Williams finished the thought.

"At the very least. There are supposedly very strict penalties for smuggling and even smoking opium in China, yet it has done very little to discourage the practice," Carol-Ann sighed.

"And how is it that you know so much about Chinese law and opium fiends, mi'lady?" Mr Bosanquent asked, looking at the young lady with a small amount of concern.

14

"Oh, Mr Bosanquent, you should know better than to ask a lady to divulge her secrets," Carol-Ann replied coyly and was rewarded with a ripple of amused laughter from all the gentlemen present.

"How long would it take to outfit a ship and send it off to anchor? Whampoa might be the ideal location to anchor at," Mr Baring said.

"I am sure that we could manage it with quickly, sir." Mr Burges replied.

"If this does prove to be profitable, then might I suggest that the single ship is replaced with large armed hulks that form a large, floating chain of opium storehouses?" Carol-Ann asked politely.

"That may be a little ambitious, my dear lady, but we shall certainly take the idea under advisement," Mr Williams chuckled.

This was the first of the dealings that Lady Carol-Ann Margaret Cowdrey-Smithe had with the East India Company, but it was far from the last.

Mr Bosanquent never discovered how it was that a young, titled lady managed to gather so much intelligence about the opium habits of a hostile nation, but as the years went by, it was not a talent that he wanted to waste.

The board of the Company had found a woman with a mind for business, a mind that placed loyalty to the Empire above individuals. This, in turn, meant that as long as the interests of the Company served the interests of the Empire, Lady Cowdrey-Smithe would be a valuable ally.

To protect her identity and to allow her to continue to gather information, as well as hold business interests of her own, Mr Baring created a new persona for the young lady – John Smith – and presented her with a pocket watch and a small chest with a tiny silver key.

"There will be things that you need to keep that will place you in a great deal of danger if they were to ever fall into the wrong hands. Keep them in this box, and keep the box hidden somewhere that no one will find it. There is space in the back of this watch for the key. Enemy agents are everywhere. If you have anywhere overseas that you can store this box when it is full, I suggest that you use it. Never let this watch out of your sight and leave a note in your last will and testament that the box should be burnt upon your death and never opened," Mr Baring told her sternly.

A marriage was arranged for the young lady to keep her in India where she could manage her own interests and those of the Company. He was a stupid man that had no real concept of anything other than his political standing.

As long as his wife maintained his position, he didn't care what she did. When her grandmother died, she gained new titles and wealth that had been held back from her father, allowing her to cement the power her husband craved and expand her own business interests, and those of the Company and the Empire.

Twenty-five years after the first ship anchored at Whampoa had grown into a fleet of large, armed hulks that served as a permanent floating warehouse. The crippling effect of the Napoleonic Wars on British silver was being compensated by the huge amounts of opium that were being smuggled into China.

The diplomatic situation in China was no less precarious than it had been when the Cowdrey-Smithe family had arrived in India. Lord Napier's son had been appointed Trade Superintendent in Canton and died only three months after taking up the post.

His loss had been a blow for the Cowdrey-Smithe family, and Lady Carol-Ann had made sure that there had been some swift retribution dealt for his death to those that she considered to be responsible for his untimely demise.

Two years after this happened, the Imperial Viceroy in Canton began to make trouble for the Company and Lady Carol-Ann. He sought to end the opium trade an executed several opium smugglers – all of whom worked for Lady Carol-Ann.

Instead of reacting with more deaths, Lady Carol-Ann ensured that the opium trade into Canton increased. However, the market in Canton was in complete chaos. Not long after the trade increased, the Viceroy seized opium chests and expelled William Jardine, an opium dealer and one of Lady Carol-Ann's business partners.

"Calm yourself, William," Carol-Ann said as the head of Jardine, Matheson & Company paced back and forth in a rage.

"Our product was seized by the hateful Viceroy, I have been expelled, and you wish me to calm down?"

William snapped.

"There is always a solution if we can let go of rage and act rationally," Carol-Ann replied.

"Well then, rationally speaking, this Viceroy is determined to make his name on stamping out opium in Canton. There is only one solution to that," Mr Jardine said, glaring at Lady Carol-Ann.

"And what is that?" Carol-Ann asked lightly.

"To protect trade in Canton, there must be war, my dear Lady de Mandeville," William said.

"If there must be war, then there is little else to be done," Lady Carol-Ann Margaret de Mandeville, Duchess of Aumale and Montagu replied, "I will make the arrangements. You will have to return to England whilst I maintain our holdings here. After you arrive, I will ensure that no one can sail from England for a few months. There are Chinese agents in London, I am certain, and if they can be uncovered, then it will make finding a weakness in this Viceroy easier."

"I shall leave it all in your very capable hands, your grace," Mr Jardine bowed slightly and left the de Mandeville Estate. Lady de Mandeville sat on her sofa for some time as she thought through all the possibilities and all the consequences of a war to secure trade in Canton.

When she was done, she stood up and walked to her writing desk, picked up a bell and rang it.

"Yes, mi'lady?" Samit said as he entered the room.

"Send for Sir Finlay. I will need him before this night is through. Tomorrow I will need you to send some letters to Mr Jardine to take to London with him, " Lady de Mandeville instructed.

"Very good, mi'lady," Samit replied and left Lady de Mandeville to think on taking the Company and the Empire to war.

Chapter 2

Lord Joshua St. Vincent was a young, cruel and ambitious man. He had been raised by a father that had more interest in fortune than sons. Lady St. Vincent was a silly woman. She was attracted to wealth, and her only desire was to be seen with as many rich and powerful people as possible in the most extravagant clothing she could find. Society and its trappings were held in the highest regard, so much so that Joshua only saw his parents once or twice a year in his youth.

The children of Lord and Lady St. Vincent had been raised by a series of governesses that were placed under the supervision of the housekeeper, Mrs Seavey. To begin with, there was only Joshua; he was the heir and treated like the king of all he surveyed.

His first governess was a young woman named Miss Harris. Her family were impoverished but came from a very good line. She was the oldest of four daughters, and though she was well-read and eminently qualified for the role of governess, her prospects for an advantageous marriage were almost non-existent. She was a plain girl without fortune.

Being plain and rich was acceptable in a wife, just as being poor but beautiful – as long as one had good breeding. Beautiful and rich young women were few and far between, so most young men had to settle for one or the other.

However, this meant that plain, educated young women, like Miss Harris, had to seek a living working as governesses in great houses that were often filled with ignorant and spoiled children.

Miss Harris had been a good governess for Joshua, she was a steady and loving influence that filled the void that his own mother left. But as more children were born to the line of St. Vincent, Joshua felt the love he had enjoyed was being stolen from him. He was a good few years older than his brother and more than a decade older than the older of his younger sisters.

Miss Harris was kept so busy taking care of all the children that she had never developed her own social life. She was isolated in the household as her position was far above the other servants, but she was never treated as an equal by Lord or Lady St. Vincent.

She spent her nights reading romance novels beside

the fireplace in her room and dreaming of a husband and children of her own.

When Joshua was sent away to school, he found himself leading groups of young boys and the thrill of being in charge. As the boys grew, they began to discover young women, and none of the serving girls at the school were safe from Joshua St. Vincent's wandering hands.

He charmed them into his bed with ease and confidence, and then cast them aside as soon as the thrill of conquest dulled and was replaced by a pallid boredom.

During the holidays he would return to the St. Vincent home and find himself consumed with jealousy over how close his siblings were to his governess.

When he was sixteen, he came home and found Miss Harris weeping in her room. She had received a letter from her father; all of her younger sisters were all now married.

The realisation that she was destined to be an old maid, taking care of other people's children until she was too old for the task and then spend the rest of her days living on the charity of her sisters whilst she cared for their children was too much for the governess to bear.

23

She was lying across her bed, her face buried in the sheets when Joshua found her. He had closed the door so quietly that Miss Harris had no idea that the young man was even in the room.

The first thing she knew of his presence was when he placed his hand on her hip as he sat on the bed beside her and whispered in her ear.

He had practised with enough servant girls to know what it was that Miss Harris wanted to hear, so much so that it was effortless for him to charm her into bed.

The affair was a rush, to begin with, he came to her room every night to have his way with the inexperienced woman that he could now possess in a way that none of his siblings ever could. It was this that made the experience exciting for him, not a notion of love.

The affair only lasted a few weeks, until Mrs Seavey discovered what was happening. Without a moments pause, she threw the governess out of the house. It was then that the parade of governesses began. No matter what woman was brought in to fill the post, when Joshua returned home from school, he seduced each of them, their age was unimportant,

24

as was their appearance.

Joshua St. Vincent's reputation became such that soon no governess would take up a position in the household whilst the threat of his ruinous influence was there. His father became so disturbed by the damage to the family reputation that he tried to send Joshua away.

He was sent to India to stay with Colonel Lewis and his brother, Callum, went with him. It was here that their paths crossed with Lady de Mandeville.

Joshua's reputation had not spread to the subcontinent, and here there were a plethora of new young women for him to seduce. When he first laid eyes on Lady de Mandeville, he saw a whole new challenge laid before him.

He could tell from looking at her that she was not like other women. She walked across a room with purpose and a sense of self that he had not seen in any woman he had met before. He saw how the men in the room reacted to her; she was an equal to some and superior to many.

She looked down on the whole room with an element of disdain, but the way she moved it was clear to Joshua that whatever room Lady de Mandeville entered, she would be in control of it.

Colonel Lewis had been keen to introduce both of the young men to the lady, and it was not long after that they began working for her.

Joshua went wherever Lady de Mandeville asked, not out of fear, but out of a desire to please her and learn how to ensnare her. It was not love, but the thrill of conquest, the same thrill that he had felt when he had first seduced Miss Harris.

But it all the years that he had worked for her, he had never been able to seduce her. Every time he received a summons to her home late at night, he was convinced that he had finally reached his goal, and each time he was left unsatisfied.

But each disappointment had only served to fuel his need to bed his employer. Yet Lady de Mandeville showed no interest in the young man. She had no use for a brash young man in her bed, no matter how useful he was in her business dealings.

Lady de Mandeville had a husband who needed a woman of seemingly pure virtue to support his political career. Any dalliances with ambitious young men of society would only serve to embarrass and derail her husband's career.

Yet her marriage was one of convenience, not affection, and it was no surprise to any that Lord and Lady de Mandeville did not have any children.

But though Lady de Mandeville was unwilling to allow young and ambitious men to share her bed, Sir Charles Finlay was quite another matter.

The youngest son of an old family, he had studied the law and come out to India to practise it, as there was no shortage of work for a student of law, no matter where in the world they found themselves.

He had worked for Jarndice & Jarndice, the legal firm that had looked after the Cowdrey-Smithe family interests and then those of the de Mandevilles. But Sir Finlay had known Lady de Mandeville for much longer than the length of his legal career.

Before Lord Cowdrey-Smithe had taken his family to India, Sir Finlay had been a playmate of Lady de Mandeville. They had run through the grounds of their homes, imagining that they were off having their own adventures of discovery in the dark jungles of India.

When Carol-Ann had been taken away to India by her family, Charles had been heart-broken. Not only had his best friend been taken from him, but she had gone to the setting of their adventures without him.

He had been told that he would forget about her in time, but this had proven to be false. He spent his childhood pretending that she was still with him. At school, he had written letters to her about what he was doing and begging for her to write back to him, but no reply ever came.

It was only when he arrived in India and found that she was married and that Lord Cowdrey-Smithe had kept the letters from his daughter that Sir Finlay understood her silence.

Her marriage had been a blow to his ego, but it had soon become apparent that all the years he had loved and missed his childhood friend he had not been alone in those feelings.

The two had fallen together almost immediately, though it had been months of being in each other's' company before they had become lovers. It was an affair that only four people knew of – Lady de Mandeville, Sir Finlay, Lord de Mandeville and Lady de Mandeville's manservant, Samit.

The pair was so discrete that Lord de Mandeville had no objections to their trysts and he was certain that the solicitor was nothing more than a much-needed distraction for his wife.

The truth of their relationship, however, was something that went far deeper than sexual pleasure. They were confidantes and a source of unwavering love and support for the other. Whatever the pair faced, whether it was an individual problem or one that confronted them both, they would find a way to solve it.

Now that she was faced with the prospect of war with a foreign power, Lady de Mandeville needed her lover now more than ever.

Chapter 3

The Canton market was not a safe place for any foreigners to walk about in. As the only place that foreigner traders could bring their wares for importing to the Chinese, one might imagine that it was a place that western influences would be welcome.

Yet, it was a far cry from any of the marketplaces that the Empire and the Company dealt in. Foreign powers were viewed as barbarians, and the inhabitants of Canton and those that sailed on Chinese ships made their views about the British people quite clear.

From across the docks, the Chinese would draw their fingers from one side of their throats to the other to indicate what would happen to any that stepped out from the market stalls and warehouses they were allowed to trade from.

After the untimely death of Lord Francis Napier, there were several successors who did not stay long in the post until Captain Charles Elliot was named as the English Trade Superintendent in Canton, though he received little guidance to help him when it came to dealing with the opium trade. Lord Palmerston, the Foreign Secretary, had given the instruction,

"It is not desirable that you should encourage such adventures: but you must never lose sight of the fact that you have no authority to interfere with or protect them."

This left Captain Elliot in a somewhat untenable position. The Chinese government wanted the trade of opium stopped, and held Captain Elliot responsible for the trade. The merchant s in Canton and even the people of Canton wanted the trade to be continued.

Though the people of Canton believed the British to be barbarians, the jobs and wealth that their opium trade brought was not something that the people wanted to lose.

There had been some small hope for Captain Elliot when Hsu Nai Tsi, one of the Chinese officials, suggested to the Emperor that the opium should be legalised and taxed in order to help with the trade deficit that the trade had created.

But the Emperor had rejected the idea.

The Viceroy of Canton was a man that was as corruptly involved in the trade of opium as any in Canton. He had been sent by the Emperor to end the trade of opium in the port, and even tried to deceive the Emperor by executing some of the Chinese opium dealers.

The Canton market was thrown into chaos, though the opium kept piling up on the ships bound for the port. The Emperor, however, was not so easily fooled and issued an imperial reprimand to the Viceroy.

It was this reprimand that led to William Jardine being expelled from Canton and some of the opium chests in Canton were seized.

It was 26th January when William Jardine boarded a ship and began his journey back to England to meet with Lord Palmerston.

Lady de Mandeville was stood on the dock watching his ship leave. She had handed over a number of letters addressed to several different people in England.

"Excuse me, your grace, Captain Elliot wishes to meet with you," a young lieutenant stammered as he approached and saluted the fearsome woman. From his uniform, Lady de Mandeville could see that he was a member of the army assigned to protect the English Trade Superintendent. There were very few men within the armed forces or the

Company's retinue that were not afraid of Lady de Mandeville and her influence.

"Very well," Lady de Mandeville said slowly as he fixed the young lieutenant with a cold look. The lieutenant wanted to scurry away from the duchess, but he had been given orders to escort Lady de Mandeville to Captain Elliot's headquarters.

It was a short walk from the harbour to the offices that Captain Elliot was working from, but even so, by the time they reached the building, the ship carrying William Jardine away from India was nothing more than a speck on the horizon.

"Your grace, thank you for coming," Captain Elliot said stiffly as Lady de Mandeville swept into his office and seated herself in one of the high-backed chairs that sat opposite the grand desk that Captain Elliot worked behind.

"I felt that it was not a request," Lady de Mandeville replied coolly.

"Indeed not. I know that you are aware of the delicate position that I am in. The Chinese are demanding an end to the opium trade, and I must maintain trade with China. We need the tea and silk," Captain Elliot began.

"We are in greater need of silver. You know what the war against Napoleon cost. We may sell the tea and silk for a profit after we have bought it from the Chinese, but that is not enough now," Lady de Mandeville interrupted.

"I cannot allow this opium trade to continue. After the seizing of the opium chests and the expulsion of Mr Jardine, I am now in a position that I must promise to clear all the opium hulks from the coast of Canton and Whampoa," Captain Elliot continued as though Lady de Mandeville had never spoken.

"Your edict does not allow you to interfere in the trade. You should be careful in exceeding your authority. You may find that your untenable position becomes a precarious one," Lady de Mandeville replied with an icy edge to her voice.

"Trade must be preserved," Captain Elliot said firmly.

"It is for that very reason that Mr Jardine has gone to Lord Palmerston. There are other ways of preserving trade that kowtowing to a nation that believes itself to be so superior to all others," Lady de Mandeville shot back.

"I will take whatever action I must to ensure that the Canton market remains open to us. Your business interests are not my concern, the overall status of our trade is," Captain Elliot sneered.

"Did it ever occur to you that my business interests are not wholly self-serving? That my actions, my interests are in fact, all in the best interest of the Empire? It is one thing to overstep your authority, but to do so with such ignorance as to the consequences is quite another," Lady de Mandeville warned.

"I did not bring you here to seek your approval," Captain Elliot frowned at the duchess.

"That is more than evident," Lady de Mandeville sighed to herself.

"I brought you here to inform you that the hulks will be cleared and no ships shall be sailing from Calcutta carrying opium. This ends now. You are to inform all those that you and your business consorts associate with that the opium trade with China will no longer continue," Captain Elliot barked. Lady de Mandeville began to laugh to herself. It was not a reaction that Captain Elliot expected, nor was it something he had ever seen before. The sight of the cold and powerful woman laughing at him filled him with a deep sense of dread.

"Do you believe that because you decree the trade is to end that it will? You have no concept of the powers at play here. And even if you succeeded in preventing any more opium being produced and shipped to China by those who share my interests, the Turkish would still produce it and ship it to China. Then all the silver that would have come flowing to us, would go to the Turks instead. Before you lose all the respect of the merchants and traders in this odd corner of the world, I would advise you to think very carefully about what it is that you are trying to achieve," Lady de Mandeville said as she stood and looked down at the captain.

"It is nothing personal, it's just business," Captain Elliot muttered.

"No one person is more important than the Empire, Charles, not me and not you," Lady de Mandeville said as she turned and made her way out of the office.

Chapter 4

Sir Charles Finlay was waiting in the library for Lady de Mandeville when she returned home. After she had sent for him and he had learned of the proposed war with the Chinese over the opium trade, he had decided that it would be best to stay at the house for some time.

"You were longer than you said you would be. What happened?" Sir Finlay frowned as he saw the look on his lover's face.

"Elliot is a fool; he is closing the opium trade in Canton to appease the Chinese. He wants the seas cleared around Whampoa, but he said nothing of Macao. We need to go to the holdings and oversee production," Lady de Mandeville sighed.

"If Elliot is clearing the estuary, then what is the point in continuing production?" Sir Finlay asked.

"He is overstepping his authority. Any promises he makes, he will have to enforce, and the Empire is in need of silver more than it is in need of appeasing a nation that will only ever view us as barbarians and beneath them," Lady de

Mandeville tutted.

"I am sure Elliot is simply trying to preserve trade with the Chinese," Sir Finlay replied, chewing his lip as he watched the duchess rifling through a stack of papers on her desk.

"Whether we trade openly or not, the hong merchants will deal with us regardless. They may not even know they are dealing with us, but we will not lose trade," Lady de Mandeville said with some level of distraction as she searched for the papers she needed.

"What can I do help?" Sir Finlay asked as he came to his lady's side.

"I need you to go to Malwa and talk to our agents there. Take this to them," Lady de Mandeville said as she handed the knight of the realm a roll of sealed parchment.

"What is it?" Sir Finlay frowned.

"Instructions as to how to proceed if things in Canton become difficult," Lady de Mandeville replied.

"You always have a plan, don't you?" Sir Finlay chuckled to himself as he took the parchment from the duchess.

"I try to plan for every eventuality," Lady de Mandeville allowed herself to smile slightly despite the frustration she was feeling.

"Whilst I am in Malwa, where will you be?" Sir Finlay asked as he took hold of Lady de Mandeville's hand.

"I will be in Bihar and Bengal," she said as she turned to look at the knight.

"Write to me?" he asked as he drew her into his arms and gazed into her eyes.

"You know that I can't. If anyone found the letters -" Lady de Mandeville began and closed her eyes as she left her voice trail off.

"One day, you will put yourself before the good of the Empire, and when you do, I will be waiting," Sir Finlay sighed sadly as he rested his head upon the top of hers.

"Be safe on your journey. Come back to me," Lady de Mandeville replied softly.

Chapter 5

The three months that followed the expulsion of Jardine from Canton were unpleasant ones. The opium trade continued in both Macao and Canton. Things for the traders were not easy though.

The Cantonese people still wanted to work with the British in the opium trade and did everything they could to keep the opium flowing from the hulks to the opium dens, but the trade was dying.

From New Year's Day, new edicts were being handed down from the Emperor. Those that smoked opium could now be executed if they were caught. The Viceroy was nervous about his own position, and in order to protect himself, he began to execute as many opium smokers as he could, in an effort to appease the Emperor.

Yet it did not stop the Emperor from sending the Imperial High Commissioner to Canton from Peking. His name was Commander Lin Tse-hsü, and he had the power to end the opium trade once and for all.

It was March when Commander Lin arrived in

Canton, and things went from bad to worse for the Company.

Commander Lin had no faith in the word of the barbarians, he was determined to end the opium trade, and unlike the Viceroy, he could not be bribed. His mission was to serve the Emperor and to end the opium trade once and for all.

News of his arrival was met with indifference from the Company and the British diplomats as they believed that he would be no different than the Viceroy.

However, the name of Lin Tse-hsü was not unknown to Lady de Mandeville, and news of his arrival in Canton was troubling to her. But not as troubling as Lin Tse-hsü arrival was to the Viceroy of Canton.

He knew that the Emperor was angry with his lack of success at halting the opium trade.

The Viceroy had formed a comfortable life for himself in the city by accepting the bribes of the opium smugglers whilst telling the Emperor that he was doing all he could to end the trade.

But now Commander Lin was coming, and the bribes

would end as would the trade that was supported by most of those living in Canton. The wealth that the opium trade was far greater than anything that the foreign trading post was used to seeing and it was due to the Company, not the Emperor.

But the Viceroy knew that it would mean nothing to the Commander. He spent days sitting in his office, making sure that the bribes he had taken could not be found by anyone looking at the records kept by the Viceroy and his staff.

When word finally arrived that the Commander was in Canton and on his way to meet with the Viceroy, the Viceroy felt he was ready to face the changing tides on which he now found himself.

His staff were busy making themselves all look indispensable for the benefit of the Commander, so the Viceroy was on his own. He was nervous as he sat, waiting for Commander Lin. He knew the Imperial High Commissioner's reputation, and he also knew that the Emperor wouldn't have sent Lin Tse-hsü if the Viceroy's conduct had pleased the Emperor.

The Viceroy was used to pressure, but the stress of the impending visit had caused him to develop a slight twitch. It was completely involuntary, but it was not the only nervous habit that he had developed.

He was confident that the bribes would not be uncovered, but there was no way to hide the perceived incompetence he had displayed at his post.

The Viceroy was only waiting an hour before there was a knock at the door.

"Come," he said. The door was opened by his secretary.

"Commander Lin Tse-hsü, Imperial High Commissioner," the secretary announced as the Commander walked into the room and looked at the Viceroy with steely eyes.

"Who are the men that are responsible for this drug flooding the empire?" Commander Lin asked. He wasted no time on pleasantries or small talk. He had no need to endear himself to a man like the Viceroy.

The Imperial High Commissioner served the Emperor and the empire and no other masters.

"There was a Mister Jardine. His company was the largest importer of opium, but I have expelled him from Canton," the Viceroy stammered. He had leapt to his feet when the Commander was announced and was now rigidly stood behind his desk.

"Yet, the problem persists. So I will ask again, who are the men that are responsible for flooding the empire with this poison?" the Commander asked in an even voice. He wasn't interested in spending any longer in the presence of the Viceroy than he had to.

Lin Tse-hsü had worked hard to achieve his high station in life. He had not been given anything he hadn't earned, and this meant that he had learned to be hard and unflinching in his attitude to his duty.

For those that tried to undermine him in the great theatre of politics had found themselves with nothing to use against him, save for the station of his birth – something that was already widely known.

He could not be bargained or negotiated with. He could not be bribed or corrupted. In the eyes of the Emperor, Commander Lin Tse-hsü was the only man that could be trusted to deal with the barbarians in Canton and bring an end to the opium smuggling that was poisoning the empire.

"Responsible?" the Viceroy stammered.

"Who are the men that, once removed, will leave the operation of these smugglers at a standstill?" Commander Lin asked, growing weary of repeating himself.

"Well, there is Mister Dent. His company is the next largest importer of opium after Mister Jardine's company," the Viceroy replied and began desperately searching through the paper on his desk. He was looking for the information that he had asked his secretary to compile on all the traders in Canton and those that could be linked to the smuggling of the drug.

He eventually found the papers he was looking for and handed them over to the Commander. Lin Tse-hsü began reading through the documents as the Viceroy hovered nervously nearby.

"Then we shall begin with Mister Dent. There is one problem though, with this plan of singling out those in Canton that are responsible," the Commander said as he finished reading through the papers.

"What is that?" the Viceroy asked, trying not to sound too worried.

"They can be replaced. As long as the supplier of this evil substance is still producing it, it will find a way to our shores. But this is a place to begin. I will need to know who the producers of this opium are. I will need your office to work from. I will need your secretary," the Commander ordered.

"And where shall I work?" the Viceroy asked.

"You shall make these arrangements and then go home until I send for you," the Commander said coldly.

The Viceroy sighed and hung his head, but nodded his agreement before he trudged slowly from the room to carry out the Commander's orders.

Chapter 6

From the moment he arrived in Canton, Commander Lin had decided that he could not trust anything that the British had to say. As far as he was concerned, they were barbarians, lesser beings that were little better than beasts and only lied.

The staff of the Viceroy worked tirelessly under the firm hand of the Commander whilst the Viceroy waited at his home in relative misery.

In his first week in Canton, the Commander laid the groundwork for seizing all the opium flooding the trade market. To begin with, he went to the Chinese and told them he was ending the trade. He warned the hong merchant that if they obstructed his will, the Commander would choose two of the merchants at random and take everything they owned.

After he was sure that the Chinese understood how seriously Commander Lin was taking the situation, he turned his attention towards the British forces. His first target was Mr Lancelot Dent of Dent and Company, but the first ultimatum was issued to all the traders in Canton through the hong merchants.

First, all opium in foreign hands, whether in storehouses, hulks or clippers are to be surrendered for destruction. Not even the smallest amount is to be withheld. Second, the barbarians must sign a bond to never import opium into the empire again. Any that do will suffer the extreme rigour of the law.

"It's beyond ridiculous!" Mr Dent exclaimed when he heard the demands, "What authority does he think he has over us to make such dictatorial demands?"

The owners of the import and trade companies, save for Mr Jardine, had all met to discuss the demands with the staff of the British Chamber of Commerce.

Captain Elliot was not there though; he was away in Macau and was still very unpopular amongst the merchants.

"John Smith sent us a message about the Commander. She seems to believe that whatever demands the Imperial High Commissioner might make are to be taken seriously. We are inclined to agree," the chair of the meeting said. He was the permanent secretary and had been given the authority to act in Captain Elliot's absence.

"Then we are simply going to acquiesce to this demand?" Dent cried.

"No, not entirely. We will try to placate the Commander. As a sign of goodwill, we shall hand over 1,000 chests of opium but continue to trade. We shall not agree to sign a bond or handing over any more opium," the permanent secretary replied.

"You think that will be enough, Sir Humphrey?" one of the traders asked.

"The Viceroy was a very reasonable man. We managed to bribe him into allowing the trade to continue. The Commander seems to simply show the Emperor he is effective in his new post. We relinquish 1,000 chests of opium, and he has instantly been more successful than the Viceroy ever was," the permanent secretary replied.

"And what if he isn't placated by your offering?" Mr Dent asked with thinly veiled frustration.

"That is not something we need to be concerned

about. Diplomacy is an art and compromise is involved on both parts – no matter how dictatorial and issued edict might be," Sir Humphrey said as he dismissed Mr Dent's concerns with a wave of his hand.

But Mr Dent remained unconvinced. He chose to walk home that evening and pondered the problems that Commander Lin could cause them all.

The permanent secretary sent the offer to Commander Lin, and to his great surprise, it was rejected out of hand. The Commander was not a man that could be bought off with a mere 1,000 chests of opium.

"Mr Dent will come to Canton. I will meet with him," Commander Lin told the envoy that had delivered the offer of the 1,000 chests of opium.

It had been four days since the demand for the opium had been issued and the Commander believed that not only was Dent refusing to meet with him but that he was playing for time by not surrendering the opium. But Dent would not enter Canton and formerly agree to the Commander's terms.

"If he refuses to come, I will bring him to the city by force," Commander Lin said. He ordered Chinese troops to assemble on the banks of the Canton River, cutting off Whampoa and the ships that sailed from the hulks to Canton, carrying the opium.

Yet, Dent still refused to come. But by 24th March, Mr Dent was no longer the target of the Commander's witch hunt. After carefully pouring over all the information that the Viceroy's secretary had compiled for him, the Commander concluded that it was not Mr Dent that he should be persecuting, but Captain Elliot.

Whilst Canton was under siege, Mr Jardine arrived back in London and petitioned for the government to take some military action to protect British trade interests abroad.

It took weeks for him to get anywhere, but he was granted a small boon in the form of agents being dispatched to gather information on the situation with more impartiality than Mr Jardine could ever hope to have.

It wasn't much, but it was enough to help the merchant to build his case of the necessity of military intervention. Telegrams and a stop on sailing were issued. The telegrams were sent to those who had served under or as an exploration officer at one time or another.

There was not a long list of individuals that were summoned to act, but it was thought best that a diverse group was sent.

Thus it came to pass that Brigadier George Webb-Kneelingroach, Miss Baker, Countess Szonja, Mr Henry Cartwright and Captain Jonnes Smith were all called to sail to India.

Chapter 7

The ship carrying the British agents arrived in Bombay in June, and they were surprised to see that Lord Joshua St. Vincent was waiting to greet them.

"Welcome to the subcontinent. The Company sent me to act as your escort. It can be easy to get lost in this city," the young lord smiled at the new arrivals, but the warmth of his smile didn't reach his eyes.

Captain Jonnes Smith stepped forward and shook hands with Joshua, but both the brigadier and countess hung back.

"What has been happening whilst we have been at sea?" Henry asked as he looked around the dock with great interest. The port seemed to be bustling with life that hadn't changed since the last time the former thief had been in the country. He had been gone for almost ten years, but the last time he had been brought to India, it had been to help in the dealings with the Hong merchants in Canton.

The exotic scents of spices and the ripe scent of manure were almost overwhelming as Lord St. Vincent led the party away from the dock and to the carriage he had waiting for them. Even in the carriage, the heat was unbearable, and Miss Baker began to understand why the clothes that Lady Sarah had arrived in England with had to be so light and breathable.

"When Captain Elliot returned from Macau he was greeted with armed junks preventing any British ships from sailing into or out of Canton. No messages could get out of the city without Commander Lin's permission. Elliot was forced to hand over all 20,283 chests of opium in Canton and promise that the British government would compensate the merchant for the loss of the opium. Once Commander Lin had the opium, he tried to force Captain Elliot to sign a barbaric bond," Joshua explained.

"What did the bond say?" Captain Jonnes Smith asked.

"That the British had to immediately withdraw from the opium trade and stop producing it. Any ship carrying opium in Chinese waters would be confiscated, and the officers on those ships would be executed by the courts of the Emperor," the young lord sighed.

"Did Elliot sign it?" Miss Baker asked.

"No, he thought it was a monstrous agreement and flatly refused. He had been doing his best to limit the trade to keep trade open with China. But they held the British in Canton hostage in order to get the chests of opium, so Captain Elliot has written to the government to intervene with military action. Jardine and the Company have already declared war on the Chinese empire, but now Elliot has written several letters to Lord Palmerston, insisting on a hard and swift strike," Lord St. Vincent said.

"What has happened to the chests of opium that were seized?" the brigadier asked.

"They have been assembling the chests at the mouth of the Canton River since April. Last week they began destroying it. The rest of the situation I shall leave to the board of the Company to explain," Joshua said as the carriage lurched forward.

They continued on their journey in silence, though it didn't take long for them to reach their destination.

They were led into a large marble building and down a long dark corridor to a room where eight gentlemen and

Lady de Mandeville sat waiting for them.

Outside the room, a distinguished looking gentleman was sat reading a book with a brown leather cover.

"Good morning, Sir Finlay," Lord St. Vincent said as he opened the door to the room and showed his guests inside.

Stepping into the room, it would have been understandable to think that they had arrived in any boardroom in London if it weren't for the heat and the open windows.

The eight men were sat in lines of four down the sides of a long thing table. Lady de Mandeville was sat at the head of the table and looked at the new arrivals with mistrust as they entered the room and took the empty seats at the far end of the table.

Those unfamiliar with the lady would not have noticed anything amiss in her countenance as she watched the new arrivals settle, not there were slight nuances in how she breathed, where she placed her hands and how long her eyes lingered on individuals that told Lord St. Vincent all he needed to know.

The young lord knew that there was a more than rocky history between the Lady de Mandeville, the countess and the brigadier, but he was not privy to the particulars.

He knew that the Egerton family, to whom the brigadier and countess were close, firmly and publicly opposed the East India Company's monopoly over trade. He assumed that this had been a point of contention between the three and that the Egerton and allies' attempts to weaken the company's vice-like grip had resulted in a negatively effecting de Mandeville's business interests. This leading to the enmity that could be seen by interested onlookers.

In truth, the young lord's suppositions were not far off the mark. But it was the Egerton's and countess' part in forcing her father to leave England for India that had been the point of contention between Lady de Mandeville and the countess.

The brigadier and Lady de Mandeville had come to blows over his wife and Mrs Webb-Kneelingroach's distaste over the growing of opium.

It was clear that Lady de Mandeville knew that opium was an evil drug that ruined lives from how she controlled the consumption of the drug amongst the Indian workforce. Yet, she still involved herself in the trade and even came up with new ways to expand it.

Mrs Webb-Kneelingroach had done all that she could to oppose Lady de Mandeville and her business enterprises. The brigadier's wife considered it corruption when Lady de Mandeville had swayed to many officers in the army, and their wives, to support and even join her enterprises.

The brigadier didn't share the same vehement opinion of Lady de Mandeville's operations whilst he was in India. But there were many deaths and unexplained disappearances that were connected to de Mandeville which soured the brigadier's view of the lady and her operations; especially when it had resulted in the deaths of Colonel Montgomery Baird and Lady Watson-Wentworth. Then the assault on his home and his ward had begun, and now the brigadier could only see Lady de Mandeville as an enemy.

"May I introduce Mr Agnew, Mr Hogg, Mr Edmonstone, Mr Alexander, Mr Bayley, Mr Ellice, Mr Astell and Mr Cotton," Lady de Mandeville said as he indicated to each of the men sat around the table, who nodded in turn.

"Welcome to Bombay. Lord Palmerston sent you to us to help with the situation we find ourselves facing. As you may have discovered so far, Commander Lin has taken a high-handed attitude that has left us very little choice, except to resort to requesting military intervention," Mr Hogg began. He saw no point in wasting any time on introductions or pleasantries.

"Then, why are we here?" Henry Cartwright asked.

"If we can gather more information and find a way to undermine Commander Lin, we may be able to avoid having to wait for military intervention to arrive, lift this embargo, and get back to making money for the Empire," Mr Cotton replied.

"Mr Jardine and Mr Dent have both told us that the Viceroy is a reasonable man who was open to bribery and was happy to allow the opium trade to go on as long as he could pretend that he was doing all he could to end it," Mr Agnew said.

"So you want information that can be used to remove Commander Lin and reinstate the Viceroy so that business can resume as normal?" the brigadier asked.

"That is precisely what we want," Mr Edmonstone replied.

"Why would the government be willing to send us to help you in such a self-serving errand," the countess asked in an icy voice.

"Since the war against Napoleon, the British Empire has been left with a shortage of silver, something that trade with China was compensating for quite beautifully. Trade is the lifeblood of the nation and any restriction of trade and sanctions that declare the British people are subject to the laws of another nation, even those who are on another continent is something that the Empire cannot allow," Lady de Mandeville replied tersely.

"Mr Smith is right; Commander Lin has made draconian demands in order to free the people that he holds hostage in Canton," Mr Ellice said.

"He is holding people hostage in the port?" Miss Baker frowned.

"He is, part of your task will be not only to find information but to also found a way to rescue those that are being held in Canton and bring them to safety in Calcutta," steepled his fingers Mr Alexander said as he leant forward and.

"Commander Lin has begun destroying the chests of opium at the mouth of the river. The stench that it has created has enforced the notion that we grow poppies on graves and feed the plants with the chopped up bodies of diseased crows," Mr said Bayley.

"They really believe that?" Captain Jonnes Smith asked with slight disbelief.

"That any some even more far-fetched notions, they consider us to be nothing more than barbarians," Mr Hogg replied.

"Have any of you had dealings with the Chinese before?" Mr Ellice asked.

"I have some contacts in Canton, amongst the hong merchants," Henry Cartwright shrugged.

The men of the board all looked at one another and then at Lady de Mandeville.

"It's why I asked for him to be sent in the letters I sent with Mr Jardine. A former thief with hong merchant contacts is much more useful than the high born in a situation like

61

this," the duchess replied glaring at the countess as she spoke.

"Then Mr Cartwright, we shall arrange to have you taken to the hulks and then as close to shore as we can take you with the Chinese blockade. You will have to make your own way to Canton," Mr Ellice said with a note of relief in his voice.

"How will I relay messages to you?" Henry asked as he avoided making eye contact with Miss Baker.

"I have informants amongst the hong merchants. They are sending me messages from other ports. But all the same, you will need to be careful. Commander Lin is fanatically loyal to the Emperor and fanaticism is a dangerous quality to deal with," Lady de Mandeville warned.

"Something you would know all too well," Countess Szonja muttered under her breath.

"Indeed I do, and a fact that you would do well to remember," Lady de Mandeville said pointedly. The countess glowered at the duchess but said nothing else.

"We have prepared quarters for you here in the city.

You should be quite comfortable there until Mr Cartwright can send us some preliminary information. Then we shall decide how to best use your combined talents to rescue the British personnel in Canton and remove this thorn from our side," Mr Edmonstone said.

Lord St. Vincent stood, which indicated that the meeting was over, and led the party from England from the room. The countess refused to look at Lady de Mandeville as she left, though she could feel the duchess' gaze burning into the back of her head.

Chapter 8

Two hours after they had met with the board and Lady de Mandeville, Henry Cartwright was ready to leave. Lord St. Vincent came to collect him, and he was taken to Lady de Mandeville.

As she was due to return to Calcutta, she had decided to take Mr Cartwright back with her along with Sir Finlay and Lord St. Vincent. Once they reached Calcutta, a small cutter was waiting to take Mr Cartwright to the hulks that floated at Whampoa. From there, arrangements had been made to see him ashore.

"Send word when you arrive," Lady de Mandeville instructed as Henry boarded the cutter. But after several weeks had passed, no word had come.

Lady de Mandeville sent a message to the hone merchants asking for a report of the arrival of Mr Cartwright, but they replied,

"Nothing to report. He has not arrived."

This caused a small ripple of panic to flow through the members of the East India Company board, but Lady de

Mandeville was not so easily alarmed. She had already begun to channel the smuggling of opium through Chusan as well as ports to the north and south of Canton.

She had plans to flood China with 8,000 chests of opium before the end of November in open defiance of both Commander Lin and Captain Elliot. Elliot was still doing his best to stop opium being taken into Chinese waters, taking depositions from the captains of ships under oath that they were not carrying opium as part of their cargo.

The disappearance of Henry Cartwright was not a great loss in the eyes of the duchess. Though his loss did make it harder for her to rescue the British that were being held hostage in Canton, she had much larger concerns.

Mr Cartwright knew nothing of Lady de Mandeville, the Company and the traders expanding their smuggling to places outside of Canton, all he knew was that they wanted to get the British people out of Canton and remove Commander Lin from his position in the city – something that even those of the meanest intelligence in Canton were already aware of.

Yet the board was not satisfied with Henry

65

Cartwright simply disappearing, so Mr Ellice and Mr Cotton paid the brigadier, countess, captain and seamstress a visit.

"Does Lady de Mandeville know you are here?" Countess Szonja asked smugly as the group sat in the comfortable seating area in the apartments that they had been given as quarters during their stay in Bombay.

"She is aware we are taking steps to find out what happened to Mr Cartwright," Mr Ellice replied.

"And these steps involve us?" the brigadier asked gruffly.

"They do. We want you, brigadier and Captain Jonnes Smith to go to Chusan and then travel south to Canton. You should be safe taking that route, though you will need to be mindful of the Chinese. They will kill you as soon as look at you. Once in Canton, you can talk to the British being held there and the hong merchants to try and find out if Cartwright is in the country," Mr Cotton said firmly.

"Is that all that you intend to do?" Miss Baker asked anxiously. She had been nervous and irritable since Henry had departed and the brigadier suspected that the pair had been conducting a love affair whilst the former thief had been renting a room from the seamstress.

"No, the gentleman departing for China is only one part of our plan. We would like you, Miss Baker, to go to Calcutta and make enquiries around the city. We have set-up a dressmakers for you, and you have some rather well-born and rich patrons waiting for you. You should be able to use it to hide your search into the crew of the cutter that Mr Cartwright sailed on," Mr Ellice said.

"And I am to remain here?" the countess asked.

"No," Mr Cotton sighed, "You, against our better judgement, are to go to Lady de Mandeville's estate. More news and information passes into her hands than anywhere else in this part of the world."

"We believe that she is keeping information from us; information coming from China, the poppy farms and even information coming from the government. We need you to stay at her home and spy on her. Any information you can gather and bring to us without her knowledge would be a great boon to us," Mr Ellice explained.

"Very well, when do we leave?" the brigadier asked to cover the countess' obvious displeasure. She had no problem spying on Lady de Mandeville, but the information she was being asked to gather would only strengthen the position of the Company. Something that Countess Szonja was not eager to do.

"Tomorrow Miss Baker, the brigadier and the captain will be taken to Calcutta. A cutter is waiting for you there, though it is one of Sir Finlay's crews so you can be certain that you will at least reach the hulks unharmed. Countess, a carriage will take you to Lady de Mandeville's estate tonight. She knows you are coming but will not be back for several days yet. She is still in Calcutta, so you will have the opportunity to look for information without fear of her discovering you," Mr Cotton said. The two gentlemen bid the four guests good day and departed, leaving the countess a short time to pack and make ready.

"Will you hand over any information to the Company?" the brigadier asked in a low voice.

"No, I won't even look for what they want. But I will take the opportunity to try and find answers to questions about the obsession that de Mandeville has with your ward," the countess replied in a whisper.

Chapter 9

Stickleback Hollow was a far cry from the exotic fields of India and the dangerous streets of Canton. They were sleepy streets of quiet country life, which were only occasionally spoilt by mystery and subterfuge.

Since the Nursery Killer had been stopped, there was little to disturb the gentle ebb and flow of village life. Lady Sarah Montgomery Baird Watson-Wentworth, Edryd Evans and Doctor Hales were in residence at Grangeback Manor, Constable Clewes was responsible for law and order in the village, and Mr Hunter, Constable Evans, Derwyn Evans, Richard Hales and Gordon Hales were off scouring the countryside for Grace Read and Millie Roy, both who had been missing for several months now.

With every passing day, it became less likely that the two women would be found at all, let alone found alive, especially as the band on ships sailing from the British Isles was soon to be lifted.

But this had not stopped the men going out to search for the two girls. They had been joined in their quest by some of the other members of the police force. The hierarchy of the Cheshire Constabulary was still in disarray as the higher ranking officer vied for Captain Jonnes Smith's position whilst he was out of the country.

This had meant that Constables Meyers, Kelly, McGill, Cantello and McIntyre were able to help search for the two women, as long as they only went in pairs.

Yet, their extensive searches had brought them no joy. There were no signs of the two women or the men that had taken them.

Mr Alexander Hunter did not like leaving Lady Sarah alone at Grangeback. The doctor had moved into the Manor in his absence as Lady Sarah was ill. She was confined to her bed, feeling weak and vomiting. Mr Hunter was worried about the young lady and had only gone searching at her urging.

He knew that she was in good hands with the doctor and Edryd taking care of her, but he wanted to be beside the woman he loved. After weeks of fruitless searching, he had returned to Grangeback and found that Lady Sarah was much better than she had been.

She was still ill, but she seemed much brighter.

"I heard that sailing has begun again," Sarah said sadly as Alex seated himself at her bedside.

"It has. The constables have sent descriptions of Grace and Millie to all the ports just in case. But I doubt they will try and leave the country now," Alex said as he took Lady Sarah's hand and gently stroked it.

"Harry will have left by now then," Sarah replied with a weak smile.

"Yes, though I am still not certain what his part in all this will prove to be. He wanted me to understand all of this before he left, say his goodbye. It was all very strange," Alex sighed and shook his head.

"There are more important things for us to be concerned with now, my love," Sarah said comfortingly.

"Your health for one thing," Alex looked at the pale lady with concern.

"That is not something for you to worry over," Sarah sighed and smiled warmly at the hunter.

"Why should I not worry?" Alex frowned.

"I am not unwell, my body is simply going through a

change for the next few months," Sarah replied and closed her eyes as she rested back against her pillows.

"A change?" Alex asked, not understanding what the lady was saying to him.

"It will not just change my life, but yours too," Sarah giggled slightly as she saw the confusion on Mr Hunter's face. She gently took hold of his hand and moved to rest on her belly as she smiled lovingly at him.

It took a moment or two for the inference to register, but as Mr Hunter grasped the meaning of the gesture, he cried out with joy and began to weep.

"I have ruined you," he sobbed.

"You have not ruined me," Sarah replied gently.

"But the scandal," Alex protested.

"Would only affect me if I wished to number amongst the society that feels it has a right to judge me," Sarah said firmly.

"Then, we must be married and soon," Alex replied with resolve.

"You want to save me from shame?" Sarah teased.

"Yes, but I would want to marry you anyway," Alex

replied as he stopped crying and smiled.

"But first you will need permission from my guardian," Sarah grinned.

"Then, until my father returns the baby and our engagement will remain a secret?" Alex asked.

"Two secrets to keep, but a lifetime of happiness for us both," Sarah replied warmly.

"A lifetime of happiness indeed," Mr Hunter agreed.

Chapter 10

Commander Lin opened the heavy door that lay before him. It was the kind of door that was designed to take effort to open. A sturdy door that was hard to break through and as hard as it was to push open, it would take even greater strength to pull open from the inside.

It was the kind of door that would withstand the pounding of enemy assaults for many days. It reminded Commander Lin of the gates to the Forbidden City, and he was glad the architect had such foresight to build such doors into the basement of the building.

He had walked down several flights of stairs to reach the doors and beyond them were several flights more. At the bottom of these stairs was a puzzle door. It was an ornate and elaborate piece of work that would take hours for any Chinaman to open if he had never seen it before, though it would be impossible for a barbarian to decipher.

It took Commander Lin moments at most to solve the puzzle and watch the door swing open. As it did, he was confronted by the sight of a man chained to the wall, his clothes torn and his torso bleeding.

He was an older man, but he was still fit considering his age. He looked up as Commander Lin entered and laughed at the sight of him.

"It didn't take long for you to get bored of waiting," the prisoner's snide remark only received a snort of derision in response.

"I do not get bored, only tired of incompetence. You are English. You were found trying to enter Canton. You are not Chinese. You do not work for the smugglers that are flooding the Empire with your poison. Who sent you?" Commander Lin replied calmly as he stood perfectly still and looked at the prisoner with a steady gaze.

The prisoner said nothing; instead, he simply stared straight ahead of him.

"What is your name?" Commander Lin asked patiently when his first question wasn't answered.

"You will answer the Imperial High Commissioner," the jailer said as he hit the prisoner over the back of the head, but not even a grunt escaped the prisoner's lips.

Instead, he simply stared straight ahead, his eyes

glazed over, his breathing slow and his demeanour serene.

"No one knows where you are. There is no point in remaining silent. You will only know life in this room for as long as you refuse to talk. You will never leave the Empire again, but how you will live here will be determined by what you can tell us," the Commander said with a slight edge to his voice.

"A prison is a prison. I was born a free man. I will die with integrity. I am no traitor," the prisoner replied.

"You will tell me whatever I want to know when the jailer is through with you. No matter how strong you believe yourself to be, everyone breaks on the third day," the Commander said firmly. He nodded to the jailer and then swept from the room.

The door slammed shut, and Henry Cartwright laughed to himself.

What have you gotten yourself into this time? he thought as the jailer began to fumble around out of Henry's range of vision.

Though he was certain that no one in India knew where he was, he was just as sure that even Lady de

Mandeville would not leave him in the hands of their enemy.

Chapter 11

The cutter slipped silently up the river. As they had sailed to the hulks and then from the hulks towards Chusan, the brigadier and chief constable saw the Chinese junks blockading Canton and patrol the estuary.

"The Imperial High Commissioner has the whole marketplace secured. Captain Elliot trying to appease the Chinese has gotten us nowhere," the captain of the ship explained to his passengers as they crept up the coast.

"I understand that Captain Elliot is very unpopular with the merchants and people trapped in Canton," Captain Jonnes Smith replied as he looked at the number of ships the Chinese had deployed and shook his head.

"He is very unpopular, but not only with the merchants and people trapped in Canton. He's becoming increasingly unpopular amongst the civil servants in India, the fleet and the British police out here," the captain snorted.

"He might be the Trade Superintendent but interfering in free enterprise and risking the lives of the British people in Canton is a fine way to make enemies," the

78

brigadier agreed.

"Yet for all the interference by Captain Elliot and the attempts by the Imperial High Commissioner to end our trading in opium, nothing is going to change," the captain sighed.

"No?" the chief constable asked.

"There is too much money to be made for the hong merchants, the Chinese people, the merchants, the Company, the British Empire and the fleet. Those who smoke the opium in the dens in China don't want to stop taking the drug either. They're threatened with death, and yet they still go to smoke it," the captain replied with a shrug.

"When it comes to money, it's not personal, only business?" the brigadier asked with an icy tone.

"Exactly, when it comes to money in these quantities, there are no laws that will remain unbroken in order to do business," the captain said dryly.

"But people are dying for this trade, for the money being made," the brigadier frowned.

"In life, every man owes one death, it is up to each one of them to decide what is worth paying that last debt for.

Some truly believe that the pursuit of silver is as good a death as any. In fact, it is better than starving in the streets," the captain replied with a sideways glance at the brigadier. From the look on his face, it was clear that the brigadier thought that the captain was wrong in his assessment, but he was not going to argue with the captain on his own ship.

Instead, the three men lapsed into silence for the rest of the journey. When they docked in Chusan, three men were waiting for the brigadier and chief constable. They were guides that had been arranged by Lady de Mandeville.

It was not an easy thing to keep secrets from the duchess, and as she could not stop the company from sending the brigadier and chief constable, she could send men in her employ to watch them.

The men led the brigadier and the chief constable out of Chusan, without anyone paying any attention to them. When they were clear of the village, they stepped off the road and made their way into the undergrowth until the shrubs, brambles and flowers masked their footprints and numbers from prying eyes.

There were plenty of men on the roads between

Chusan and Canton, but none of them saw the party that snuck by them in the flora. Some wore military uniforms, others looked like refugees and then there were those who looked like merchants, but with the disappearance of Henry Cartwright, none of the group creeping to Canton trusted anyone that was not in the employ of the merchants, the Company or Lady de Mandeville.

As they neared the city, the guides took the men down towards the water's edge.

"We swim," was all the guides said. They all stripped down to their underwear and placed their clothing in leather sacks that were then strapped to their waists.

The water was icy cold as they slipped into it and began the slow swim into the city. They waited until dark to begin their swim, the guides sticking close to their two charges as they navigated the waterways.

The junks that blockaded the city were not looking for swimmers, so there was little risk of the party being spotted. However, if the five men had been seen in daylight attempting to swim up the river, it would have seemed highly suspicious.

The water rippled, but the swimmers barely disturbed the water, none of them daring to cause a splash in case it drew the attention of those guarding the harbour.

When they passed by the junks, the guides turned towards the docks, and the men began the more treacherous part of the journey – swimming between the moored ships in the harbour.

By the time they reached the docks where the merchants were waiting for them, the five men were so tired and cold they could scarcely breathe.

"We must be quick; a patrol will be by soon. Clothes and a warm fire are waiting for you at the warehouse," one of the merchants said.

The five men were herded quietly from the edge of the docks and into one of the long warehouses that belonged to Mr Dent.

Inside it was pitch-black, save for a few pinpricks of light that were leaking from around a doorway further in.

The men were led to the door and quickly ushered inside. On the other side of the door, two men in fine clothes were pacing about whilst four others sat by the fire waiting patiently.

"Thank God, you're here at last!" one of the finely dressed my cried and came over to drag the brigadier and the chief constable over to the fireside.

The fire was a welcome relief as the men were shivering in the cold of the night. Their clothes were exchanged for warm towels, and dry clothes which included large boat cloaks to help keep the chill out as they sat by the fire.

"We received word you were coming from some of the hong merchants that are still willing to defy Commander Lin. We've been waiting for several hours. We thought for certain you'd be captured," the other finely dressed man blabbered with relief as he sat with the brigadier and the captain. The guides that had brought the two men safely into Canton had gone back to their homes now that their task was complete.

They were men that worked for the British, but they had no need to be part of the conversations that were about to take place.

"Have you heard anything about the fate of Mr Henry

Cartwright?" the brigadier chattered as he rubbed his arms and hoped this would be the last time he would have to risk life and limb for Queen and country.

"Nothing so far, but it is not safe for us to venture outside of our trade areas. The Chinese consider us to be barbarians and would think nothing of slaughtering us like animals in the street," the first man said sadly.

"But the men that guided us here were Chinese," Captain Jonnes-Smith frowned.

"Yes, but there are few that are as loyal as those that are paid by Lady de Mandeville. Her reputation is something that most of us can only aspire to you. They wouldn't dream of betraying her. The penalties of betraying the Chinese Emperor are severe, but the penalties of betraying Lady de Mandeville are far worse," the second man replied.

"But not all of Canton is under her control?" the brigadier scoffed.

"If it were, the Commander would have mysteriously disappeared as he entered the city and none of this would be happening. There are rumours that she has already begun to shift the opium trade to other cities and towns on the coast. It will cause the Commander a great deal of embarrassment and show the Emperor that Lin has failed just as miserably as his predecessors," the second man said.

The four men that had been sat around the fire had withdrawn and now stood on either side of the door to the warehouse.

They had hung the wet underwear on wooden frames by the fireside and undone the leather parcels to warm the clothes that they contained before they had withdrawn.

"We need to head out into the city and see what we can learn about Mr Cartwright's whereabouts," the chief constable said firmly.

"No, you'll end up floating in the river, and no one in power in Canton will care. If you need to gather information, I suggest we use Lady de Mandeville's agents. They can bring the people you need to talk to to meetings after dark. We can change the locations and ensure that if Commander Lin's men hear about them that there are plenty of warnings in place to help you flee before you can be arrested," the first man said.

"I must apologise for my rudeness, but we don't even

know your names, how can we trust your judgement?" the brigadier grunted.

"Where are our manners? In all this cloak and dagger, protocol quite escaped us. May I make amends with introductions? I am Mr Simon Marsh, and this is Mr Peter Smith. We are associates of Mr Dent and Mr Jardine. We are the most senior merchants of those trapped here in Canton, and as such, we feel responsible for the lives of those that are trapped here with us. That includes yourselves and Mr Cartwright," the second man explained.

"Then you have both been in Canton for some time?" Captain Jonnes Smith asked.

"Far longer than either of us wished to be, but we are certain that meeting contacts after dark in a number of locations would be much safer for you both than moving through the markets in the day," Mr Smith replied.

"Then we will bow to your knowledge for now. Time is short, and if this method doesn't bear fruit, we will try it our own way," the brigadier said firmly.

"Very well, we'll send for your guides in the morning. We have prepared some quarters for you above the warehouse, when you are ready, these men will take care of you. There is food waiting for you in your rooms. We must be heading home now before we are missed," Mr Marsh said and bid the chief constable and brigadier goodnight.

Chapter 12

Countess Szonja was woken by the carriage jolting to a stop at the estate of Lady de Mandeville. The journey to the estate had been a long one that had left the countess feeling drained.

She hated travelling long distances without stopping at decent inns, something that she had to forgo in India. The horses were changed at different outposts, but they were military in their usage and had nowhere suitable for the countess to rest, and the food was little better than marching rations.

As the carriage stopped outside the main house, a man came down to meet her. He was a native of India, but he was dressed in a white suit and beside him walked an unmistakably British man dressed in a uniform that the countess didn't recognise.

The native man opened the door to the carriage and bowed to the countess.

"Countess, it is a pleasure to welcome you. My name is Samit, I am the head of the household for Lady de

Mandeville and am here to ensure that your stay here is as comfortable as possible," the native man said with a smile.

"Thank you, Samit," the countess said as she stifled a yawn.

"May I also introduce Superintendent Geoff Crump. He is the head of the British Police here in the Calcutta province," Samit said as he stepped back slightly and let the superintendent come forward to greet the lady.

"A pleasure, countess," Superintendent Crump said and helped the countess out of the carriage.

"Thank you, superintendent," Szonja smiled as warmly as she could.

"I have prepared a room for you to refresh and relax in after your journey. The duchess is due to return in three days, so your time is your own until then. I will happily provide you with a tour of the estate whenever you like. The superintendent is staying here until the duchess returns as well. Dinner will be served at 7pm, but I will have a light lunch brought to your rooms in a few hours when you have had time to rest," Samit said and led the way into the grand house.

"Thank you, Samit," the countess said as she was shown to her room.

"If you need anything, then please ring the bell beside your bed," Samit said as he bowed and left the countess alone.

The countess knew that she didn't have much time until Lady de Mandeville returned, but she couldn't resist lying down on the bed after her long journey, and very soon, she was asleep.

When she awoke, she found a tray had been brought in to her room, it was covered with a selection of cakes and sandwiches that the countess would have expected to find in the tea rooms of London rather than an estate in India.

She sat up and rang the small silver bell by the bed. A few moments later, Samit opened the door carrying a full silver tea service.

"I thought it best to bring the tea once you were awake," Samit smiled as he placed the tea service down beside the tray of food.

"Thank you, Samit," the countess replied as he poured out the tea for her, placed the cup and saucer on the tray of food and carried them over to the bed for her.

"You are most welcome. I am told that we share an acquaintance," Samit said as he carefully placed the tray on the bed. It had legs that allowed it to stand over the countess' lap so that she could eat and drink without fear of spilling the contents of the tray all over the bed.

"Oh?" the countess asked with surprise.

"I grew up with the Lady Montgomery Baird Watson-Wentworth as she is now known," Samit said with a wisp of a smile at the memory.

"I see, then we do share an acquaintance," the countess said carefully as she sipped her tea.

"I am aware that I am not in a position to enquire after her health, but it would be a great comfort for me to know that she is well and that the attempts of certain parties to harm her have failed," Samit said as he bowed and walked to the door of the countess' room.

"Her ladyship is well. She is a woman of friends and resources," the countess said as she studied Samit over the rim of her cup.

"Thank you," Samit sighed, his shoulders relaxing

with relief. He closed the door quietly behind him, and the countess began to think that the head of the household could be quite useful to her.

Chapter 13

The boat arrived in Calcutta three days later than scheduled. It had not been an easy journey from England to India, but Mr Harry Taylor was relieved to finally reach land.

He had clutched the pocket watch rather tightly to him throughout the journey, never letting go of it, even when he was asleep.

Harry had expected a carriage to be waiting for him when he arrived in Calcutta, but instead, Sir Finlay was stood there with a grave expression on his face.

Mr Taylor followed the knight of the realm through the streets of the port and up to a rather shabby looking building.

The door was guarded by a cruel-looking man that the people on the street were taking great pains to avoid passing too close to.

The guard nodded to Sir Finlay and let Harry and his escort pass into the building unaccosted. After climbing several flights of stairs, Sir Finlay showed Mr Taylor into a small room where there was nothing but a single chair, upon which, Lady de Mandeville was sat.

"Did you bring it?" the lady asked as Sir Finlay shut the door to the room.

Harry took the pocket watch out of his coat and handed it over without a word. Relief spread over the face of the lady as she took the watch out of his hand and carefully examined it.

"Well done," she said approvingly as she turned it over and popped open the back of the watch. As her eyes fell on the works of the watch, Lady de Mandeville's face fell.

She slowly looked up from the watch and at Mr Taylor with a snarl on her face.

"Where is it?" she asked acidly.

"Where is what?" Harry asked with a worried expression plastered across his features.

"The key that was in the back of this watch. Where is it?" Lady de Mandeville asked, her voice barely above a growl.

"I don't know. I didn't open the watch. I didn't know about the key. It hasn't been out of my hand since I reclaimed it from Hunter," Harry stammered.

94

"Then they have it, and you have failed me," the duchess shook her head and sighed heavily as she weighed up the young gentleman's future in her mind.

"I retrieved the watch; I knew nothing of any key," Harry protested.

"If you had retrieved the watch when you first were given the task, they wouldn't have found the key. I have no further use for you here. But there is a task for you in Canton," Lady de Mandeville said with a dark look on her face.

"Canton? You're sending me to China?" Harry blanched at the thought.

"That is where you are needed now. The Company has tried to move without my consent. You are going to address the balance of power that has been upset. You will not be going alone, but you are going to Canton," Lady de Mandeville said as she slowly rose from the chair and sauntered past Mr Taylor.

"Very well, your grace. When do I depart?" Harry sighed sadly.

"In the morning, you will spend tonight at the estate.

We are going there now. We're not expected for three days, but I have another guest that I need to watch," the duchess said curtly and made her way to the door.

Harry shook his head and hoped that he wouldn't be in exile in China for too long. He had expected not to return to England after retrieving the watch, but that had been before he knew that he had failed.

He only had moments to contemplate his situation as the sound of Lady de Mandeville's footsteps echoing down the corridor accompanied by Sir Finlay's told him that he had to follow or else be left behind.

Chapter 14

Lord Joshua St. Vincent sat his rooms in a small apartment in Calcutta. He had been waiting in the port since the departure of Mr Henry Cartwright for China.

Lady de Mandeville had issued him no further instructions since he had been ordered to act as an escort. She had sent for Callum St. Vincent but seemingly had no use for the older brother.

This had proven to be quite fortuitous for the young lord. He had other matters that he wanted to attend to that he didn't want Lady de Mandeville interfering in, at least not yet.

He had been waiting for two days when something he had been longing for was delivered to him. It was a small box that was made from mahogany and polished so that it shone as the young lord unfolded the soft white cloth from around the box.

To the untrained eye, it looked like something akin to a jewellery box, but it was much heavier to lift.

The lock on the box was small and intricate, but it

took Joshua mere moments to open it using the picklock he had acquired on his last visit to London.

The lock gave way and the lid to the box popped open. He carefully opened the lid and saw that the box was lined with felt and filled with papers.

He carefully took out the first of the papers; it was dated just a few months ago and dealt with the opium situation in Canton. The paper contained the names of all those that dealt in the trade both for the British and for the Chinese.

Next, there were papers that listed who each of the poppy fields in each province belong to, the names of the farmers and those that had been coerced into growing the drug instead of growing anything else.

The more he read, the more Lord St. Vincent understood how imperative the opium markets in China were to Lady de Mandeville's plans and to the fortunes of the Company and the British Empire.

Contained in this box was all the information that was needed for an ambitious man to not only topple the legend of John Smith, but also to unravel the power of the Company and the British Empire.

Each piece of paper was older than the last, and each one contained more secrets that brought a devilish smile to the lips of the young lord.

The papers went back decades, and when he had finished reading them, he knew exactly what he was going to do.

He placed all of the papers neatly back in the box and sat in his chair, contemplating his future. In the box beside him was the power to inspire uprising in India and end all British trade in the East if Lady de Mandeville didn't bow to his wishes. Lord St. Vincent found the idea so delightful he couldn't help but smile to himself before he made plans to travel to the de Mandeville Estate.

Chapter 15

The de Mandeville Estate was filled with activity when Lord St. Vincent arrived. Lady de Mandeville, Sir Finlay and Mr Harry Taylor had not been at the estate long when Lord St. Vincent's carriage pulled up at the main house.

Callum St. Vincent had arrived an hour before Lady de Mandeville, and with the superintendent at the house, it had been impossible for the countess to search for information she wanted.

She knew there would be some opportunities to search Lady de Mandeville's study, but with so many people in the house, it would prove more useful to listen at doorways to see what she could discover.

No one in the house seemed to pay much attention to the countess' presence. Lady de Mandeville had no desire to greet the guest that the Company had foisted on her, and she had more pressing matters to deal with.

Harry and Callum both knew that they were to be sent to Canton and neither was thrilled by the prospect of sneaking into the city, especially after the disappearance of Henry Cartwright. The pair had greeted each other warmly and then taken to walking in the rose garden to discuss what they had both heard of conditions in China.

Sir Finlay had taken the superintendent to the billiard room to enjoy a relaxing game whilst the pair discussed the varying legal differences between England and India. It was a well-worn conversation that the pair were always keen to indulge in, but not something that anyone else was willing to listen to or participate in.

Lady de Mandeville was sat in her study, going over some papers and reports that had been placed upon her desk in her absence. She had thoroughly checked the room to ensure that nothing had been disturbed by unwelcome hands rifling through them, but everything was as it should have been.

She was almost feeling relaxed when there was a rapping at her study door.

"Come," she ordered without looking up from the reports she was reading.

The door slowly creaked open, and Lord St. Vincent

stepped into the room. In his hand, he carried a rough sack that seemed to contain something very heavy.

"Your grace," the young lord said in greeting as he walked over to her desk and sat in one of the chairs that face it.

"And what brings you here without an invitation?" Lady de Mandeville asked coldly without looking up from the papers she was studying.

"I am your humble servant, as always, your grace, but I have discovered something that I felt that I should bring to your attention," Joshua replied with a slimy demeanour. The tone of his voice made the duchess pause in her reading and glance up at the young lord.

There were certain elements of human behaviour that she had learned to judge in a moment, whether for weakness or danger, her instincts had served her well. The sound of triumph that rang in Lord St. Vincent's voice was an instant warning of danger that she knew better than to ignore.

"And what is that?" she asked as she slowly put down the reports and sat up straight in her chair. Her eyes carefully weighed Joshua as he looked at her with a satisfied grin on his face.

The young lord opened the sack he was carrying and slowly lifted out of it a heavy item that was wrapped in a white cloth.

He carefully placed the item on the desk in front of the Duchess of Aumale and Montagu and gently pulled the white linen aside to reveal a box that Carol-Ann knew every well.

She sat for a moment, simply staring at the box. Her hands were still and her face a placid mask that betrayed none of the anger she felt at being confronted with the offending item.

The box had been well hidden, and only an act of betrayal from one of her most trusted allies would have seen the box into the hands of a man like Lord Joshua St. Vincent.

Her mind whirled as she considered the consequences of him knowing what the box contained. She could see the lock had been picked and the contents, though replaced, were now peeking out through the open box lid.

"I see. This is indeed something that needed to be brought to my attention," she replied just as coldly as before,

"What action did you intend to take?"

"There were several things I considered, but I think I have decided on the best course of action," the young lord smirked as he looked at the icy face of his employer.

"I see and what course of action is that?" Lady de Mandeville asked as she rose from behind her desk and slowly walked around to stand between Joshua and the box.

Joshua slowly drew his eyes up and down her body as she stood there, silently appraising her body before he stood and grabbed her by the waist.

"I know all the dirty little secrets you have," he whispered in her ear, "I can ruin you as easily as I can snap my finger, but there is no fun in simply destroying a creature as rare and fine as you are,"

His voice made her skin crawl, but she controlled her revulsion and managed to remain still in his arms.

"Then pray tell, where does the fun lie?" Carol-Ann asked, already knowing the answer she was about to receive. Joshua chuckled to himself as he ran one of his hands slowly down from her waist and rested it on her skirt between her legs. The flimsy material of her sari let his fingers move much

104

closer to her body than the clothes that she would have worn in London would have allowed, and she shuddered slightly as she felt his fingers exploring her body.

"You will come to my bed; you will become mine and mine alone. I will have complete control over you, your business contacts and the direction of the Company and the Empire. Then when I have had my fill of you, we shall have to renegotiate," Lord St. Vincent snarled as he dug his fingers into her waist and began to pull up her sari.

"This is hardly the place for you to begin enjoying your new property," the duchess gasped and managed to worm her way free of his clutches.

"Then what does your grace suggest?" Lord St. Vincent asked as he greedily watched her move across to the drinks tray. She poured a glass of whisky and drained it almost immediately before pouring another.

"A toast to a new future, then you shall have whatever you desire," the lady sighed in defeat.

"I prefer port to whisky," Joshua instructed as he sat down and watched the powerful businesswoman pouring out a drink for him.

"To the future," she said quietly as she walked over to where the young lord sat and handed him the small glass filled with rich red liquid.

"I have never seen you drink this port, and I always wondered when I would get the opportunity to taste it. It seemed to me that it must be something that you saved for only your most important business associates," Joshua grinned as he opened his mouth and quickly drained the glass.

Lady de Mandeville took the glass from his hand and moved to the fireplace in the room. It was something that seemed out of place in a country that was always so warm, but it was a necessity for burning unwanted papers and disposing of other items.

She threw the glass at the back of the fireplace and watched the crystal shatter into thousands of tiny shards.

"You are right, it is a very special bottle, but one that I have rarely had the occasion to use. You will begin to feel rather dizzy soon, and your vision will blur. You may already feel the sapping of your strength and an inability to move that will make your last few hours rather unpleasant.

You see, one of the wonderful things about India is the availability of some many venoms and poisons. What you have consumed is my own concoction, something that I will not bore you with the details of, but it is very effective at paralysing and poisoning, ensuring a long and painful death.

"In fact, I have never been able to discover whether it is the poison or suffocation that those who drink it die from. Though, I suppose that you won't be able to tell me which, so it is rather a moot point. I always knew there would come a point when you outlived your usefulness. You always have been far too – precocious – for your own good. Your appetites have been your undoing though; they have always blinded you so, made you very easy to control. You may be wondering why I couldn't simply live with you controlling me. I doubt you will understand, but none of this has ever been about me," Lady de Mandeville said as she carefully shut the lid of the box on her desk and pulled the white linen over it.

"I am and always have been a servant of the Empire. I have been blessed by God with skills that are of use to the Empire and have placed me in a position of guardianship. I cannot let anyone control me. Everything I do, I do for the good of the Empire, not myself and one life is not worth more than the millions that I have guardianship over. You shouldn't worry; you'll be given a gallant death in the reports. Something that will ensure your family name isn't shamed by this tawdry attempt at blackmail. Besides, I am sure that your brother will make a much more fitting Lord St. Vincent than you ever could of," she sighed with satisfaction.

Outside the room, in the corridor, Countess Szonja slipped silently away to her room.

Chapter 16

The countess sat in her room in shock. She had always known that the duchess was a ruthless woman, but had never fully understood what lengths she was prepared to go to or what her driving motivations were.

It was true that many men and women professed to doing all that they did for the glory of the Empire, but these words often rang hollow, especially when their actions proved to be solely self-serving.

But Lady de Mandeville had no way of knowing that Szonja was in the hall, listening to everything that was going on in the room, watching through the keyhole. The only person that she was talking to was a man that she had killed.

There was no reason for her to lie to a dead man or to even explain to him why he had to die. Yet, she had taken the time to explain what fate awaited the young man and why he was such a fool to cross her.

The countess had always disliked the duchess, not merely because she was a strong woman who succeeded in the world of business, but because she had always imagined that the duchess sought more power for herself.

This revelation of such selfless intentions, though accompanied by delusions of grandeur, was enough to give Szonja pause to not only consider her purpose for being on the estate but her whole opposition to Lady de Mandeville and her plans.

She sat by the window and looked out at the grounds as she became lost in thought. The countess was so consumed by her thoughts that she didn't hear the footsteps approaching her room or the door to it being opened.

The first thing she knew of another being present in her room was the dull thud of something being placed firmly on her dressing table.

"Lady de Mandeville, I'm sorry, I didn't hear you come in," the countess stammered as her heart fluttered in her chest. The sound of a heavy box being placed on her dressing table had startled her, but the presence of her hostess was far more terrifying, especially after what she had just witnessed.

"You seemed to be contemplating something important, though this may be somewhat more important to you," the duchess said coolly as she uncovered the box.

"And what is this?" Szonja asked innocently.

"Every keyhole has an eye and every wall ears. My maid told me that you were stood outside my study just now. Please do not waste any time by trying to deny it. You were sent here to spy on me, something that I am sure you took great pleasure at being asked to do. What you overheard in my study may warrant some explanation," Carol-Ann said brusquely,

"And what explanation is it that you care to give me?" the countess asked as she peered curiously at the box.

"This box contains everything that the late Lord St. Vincent was trying to use as blackmail leverage. If you wish to read all contained within, you will be in the same position that he was. You have seen what happens to those who try to blackmail me and you heard the motivations of my blackmailer. Though we have always been on opposite sides, this may help you understand my position better, and why what I have done has been done for the good of the Empire," Lady de Mandeville said as she turned on her heel and left the countess alone with the box.

Szonja waited until the duchess had gone, and the door to her room was firmly closed before she rose to examine the chest. It seemed strange to her that something that was clearly damning for Lady de Mandeville should be so readily offered to her.

She understood the duchess' threat of death well enough, but in England, there were limits as to what Lady de Mandeville could do to the Countess of Huntingdon.

As long as Szonja kept what she learned to herself whilst she was in India, she was not in any immediate danger.

Though she didn't understand the logic of the duchess, she was curious as to what kind of information the chest contained. To have such power over a woman like Lady de Mandeville, the countess could only imagine how terrible the secrets were.

She picked up the first of the papers and began to read. As she read, her brow became furrowed. She moved onto the next paper and the next. The more she read, the more she understood what actions the duchess had taken in the East to secure the hold of the Empire not only for trade but a stable occupation that benefited the British people and those that had submitted to British rule.

It wasn't just India that this applied to, but the rest of the Empire as well. Every corner that the British had conquered and named as a colony was secured through the actions that Lady de Mandeville had laid down, at least in the political and civil spheres.

By the time the countess had finished reading all the documents, she understood the duchess' reasoning for letting her read the documents. She folded each one back up and replaced them in the box.

There were many rumours about the Company and of the activities of John Smith, but reading through the files in the box made all of them seem to be nothing but opposition propaganda.

The countess sat for a while, thinking of all the things she had been told, everything she thought she knew of the duchess and everything she now knew.

It was now very clear why Lady de Mandeville had gone to such great lengths to procure the key that Mr Hunter had found in the pocket watch that Lady Sarah's parents had stolen.

But it raised some rather alarming questions in the countess' mind.

Who had Colonel Montgomery Baird and Lady Watson-Wentworth been working for when they stole the pocket watch? If they knew that they were going to die, why had they risked the life of their daughter to bring the pocket watch to England? And why had Lady de Mandeville been unable to retrieve the pocket watch before it had left India with Lady Sarah?

Chapter 17

The journey for Mr Taylor and Mr St. Vincent was much the same as the journey that the brigadier and Captain Jonnes Smith had experienced.

Lady de Mandeville's Chinese agents met the two men in Chusan and guided them to Canton, using the river to swim into the port during the dead of night.

Though it was the brigadier and chief constable that brought warm clothes and provided a fire to the two new arrivals rather than Mr Marsh and Mr Smith.

However, the meeting of old adversaries in such a place was far from cordial. The Chief Constable had no prejudices against Mr Taylor or Mr St. Vincent, but for the brigadier, they were the last two men that he had wanted to see in Canton – or anywhere for that matter.

When the two newcomers were warm and dry, the brigadier had moved away from them both and staunchly refused to speak a word to either.

"Come now, George, we are all here on common purpose," Captain Jonnes Smith had tried to cajole some form of camaraderie from the brigadier towards his adversaries.

"They are here on behalf of a woman that killed some of my dearest friends, and these two men have tried to harm my ward on the orders of that woman. There is no common purpose," the brigadier replied gruffly.

George was not happy that he had to deal with the two young men being in Canton, but as long as they were with him, they could not harm Lady Sarah.

It was around midnight when Harry and Callum arrived at the warehouse, and both men were in dire need of rest. The brigadier spent what remained of the night sitting by the door of the room the two young gentlemen slept in, making sure that neither man left and that the brigadier could listen to any conversation that passed between them.

But there was no conversation to overhear, and there was no bid for escape from either man. When the dawn broke, the brigadier was in a foul mood from lack of sleep and was in no state to humour anyone with conventional niceties.

There was no time for him to sleep either as people

came to the warehouse throughout the day with different messages and information that they had gleaned from contacts in the marketplace and bribing officials that were less than enthusiastic about Commander Lin's regime.

Captain Jonnes Smith did his best to welcome Harry and Callum to Canton, despite George's disagreeable attitude. The chief constable was unaware of most of the intrigue that his three compatriots had been involved in over the past few months, and so he had no reason to dislike the two young gentlemen.

So the brigadier spent the day sitting on an uncomfortable stool with his arms folded, listening to all the agents that brought information to the warehouse but not uttering a word to anyone.

At midday, Mr Marsh paid a visit to the warehouse and brought with him the news that more soldiers had arrived and that the stench of the opium being destroyed was only getting worse.

He stayed for a few hours, but there was nothing of interest until an hour before the sunset.

One of the agents that had brought the men safely

into Canton came to the warehouse with information that wasn't simply the movement of troops and the morale of people in the city.

"Henry Cartwright, I know where he is," the man said in broken English.

"Where?" the chief constable asked urgently.

"Commander Lin has him," the agent replied.

"But where is he?" the brigadier asked with irritation.

"The man didn't say. He will take us there after dark," the agent said.

"Who is this man?" Harry asked with suspicion.

"He works for the Viceroy. He doesn't like Commander Lin," the agent replied.

"The enemy of my enemy is my friend?" Callum scoffed with slight disbelief.

"We go after dark to meet him. He will take us to Henry Cartwright," the agent said firmly and then left without another word.

"It must be a trap. There is no reason for anyone that works for the Viceroy to help us," the brigadier said gruffly.

"The people of Canton make a lot of money from the

opium trade, they stand to lose as much as the Company and the Empire if Commander Lin is successful," the chief constable countered calmly. He knew that the brigadier was in a foul mood, but he wasn't going to let a bad temper cloud their judgement if there was even the smallest chance that they could find and rescue Henry.

"You think we should meet with this man?" Callum spluttered.

"I do, it may be a trap, but Commander Lin is not a man of subterfuge. He is a man of direct action as his demands and actions demonstrate. He wouldn't believe for one moment that anyone has managed to sneak into Canton, let alone that there is anyone looking to free his prisoners," Captain Jonnes Smith replied.

"Very well, then we will go to the meeting. The worst that can happen is that we end up imprisoned with Mr Cartwright," Harry replied dryly.

"Then at least half of our mission will have been accomplished," the chief constable replied with a wry smile.

"We should all get some rest, I fear it is going to be something of a long night," the brigadier yawned and took the opportunity to leave the three men to argue whilst he slept for a few hours.

He knew that the meeting was most likely a trap, and if they were going to walk into it, George wanted to be well-rested.

Chapter 18

The brigadier was woken by the chief constable shaking his shoulder. It took a few moments for George to remember where he was and why he was there, but when he did, he rolled out of the uncomfortable cot and stretched out his ageing back.

Every moment that he was in China, he was feeling his age more and more.

"This really is a young man's game," he muttered to himself as he felt the muscles in his back and legs complain.

He slowly made his way down the stairs from the upper floor of the warehouse to the ground floor where the others were waiting for him.

Mr Taylor, Mr St. Vincent and Captain Jonnes Smith were waiting with the agent and Mr Marsh for the brigadier when he finally made it down the stairs to the ground floor of the warehouse.

The agent had brought with him a range of weapons that were little more than sticks for the men to choose from, as it seemed that they would not be going to the meeting unarmed.

"Still believe that we are walking into a trap?" the chief constable asked with a smug grin as the four men inspected the weapons.

"Yes, giving us these could be a way to make us feel more comfortable, and they end up shooting us before we get close enough to use these things," Harry replied shortly.

He had been in a bad temper since he had discovered his failure and learned that his punishment was being sent to Canton. The only way he could redeem himself in his employer's eyes was to survive his almost certain death sentence and help all those that were being held hostage in the city by Commander Lin.

But this had not caused his foul mood. The reason for it was his own failure and belief that he had outsmarted Mr Hunter in taking the pocket watch from him without realising there was more to reclaim than the watch itself.

He was annoyed that the key had been discovered and that he hadn't checked the watch himself when he obtained it. The moment that Lady de Mandeville had opened the back of the watch, it was obvious that something belonged on top of the works and was missing.

His overconfidence had led him to his current predicament, and it was a mistake that he never wanted to make again.

Following an agent that they had only met a few times to a meeting with an unknown person armed only with a stick. Only Captain Jonnes Smith seemed to be comfortable with their current course of action, something that worried Harry considerably. To him, it seemed the chief constable was reliving his glory years as they skulked about under Commander Lin's nose.

But as long as Mr Taylor remained wary of their guide and his surroundings, he knew he stood a good chance of surviving whatever Canton had to throw at him,

The port itself was almost in total darkness as Mr Marsh waved the five men off into the night. The agent led the way, closely followed by Captain Jonnes Smith and Mr St. Vincent. The brigadier and Mr Taylor walked at the back of the group, neither man trusting the other to walk behind them.

Soldiers patrolled the streets, but the men's guide

knew the patrol schedules and places where the five men could hide as the soldiers passed by. It seemed to Callum that they had been moving for hours as their progress was so slow. The agent took great care to ensure not only did they pass unobserved by the soldiers, but by the citizens of Canton as well. However, this meant that an otherwise quick journey seemed to drag on into eternity.

When they finally arrived at the meeting place, it seemed to be deserted.

"It's looking more like a trap again," Harry muttered as he shifted the stick in his hands. They had stopped at the meeting point of five alleyways, and there wasn't a soul in sight. There was nowhere to hide, and it would be easy to surround the five men and cut off any hope of escape.

"On the contrary, if it had been a trap, you would have been sent straight to Mr Cartwright's location and been captured yourselves," an accented voice spoke from the depths of the alley shadows.

"Who's there?" Callum called out. In reply, the owner of the voice stepped into the centre of the alleyway meeting point, where a small lamp was swinging from one of the buildings, casting a small ring of light.

"This is the Viceroy of Canton," the agent said as he bowed low to the official.

"Your English is excellent," the brigadier said as he bowed slightly, offering the Viceroy a small show of respect.

"I have had many dealings with your merchants. Speaking your language well has proven useful," the Viceroy replied.

"And why should we not consider this to be a trap?" Harry frowned at the Viceroy, bringing an end to the polite portion of the conversation.

"What reason do I have to trap you? Commander Lin has been brought to replace me. I have lost power and money. I have nothing to do but sit at my home and wait for the Emperor to order my execution for my failure. If I can cause the Imperial High Commissioner to become disgraced as a worse failure, the Emperor's wrath will be turned from me, and I will be returned to my former station. I have no reason to support Commander Lin in his quest to rid the Empire of opium," the Viceroy replied coldly.

"And freeing our friend will be a factor in his

disgrace?" Callum asked.

"A man that is scheduled to be executed for crimes against the Empire disappears whilst opium is still flooding into my country through other ports? It is more than enough to shift where the Empire's ire is focused," the Viceroy replied.

"Executed?" the brigadier echoed.

"The order arrived from the Emperor this morning," the Viceroy said with indifference. He had no love for the barbarians and no desire to be allied with them for longer than he needed to be. For the moment they were useful in his bid to remove Commander Lin, and the gold of their merchants was useful for maintaining his lifestyle, but he would happily turn on the barbarians if handing them over to the Emperor served his purpose.

"And that is enough to persuade you to help us?" the chief constable sounded sceptical.

"Of course not, but I have always been well compensated for my co-operation by Mr John Smith, and his agent assures me that once you are safely out of Canton, I shall be even more richly rewarded than I have been before," the Viceroy replied with a grin.

"A greedy man out for revenge is always easy to trust. His motivations are simple, and it is rare for greed to trounce revenge," the brigadier said dryly.

"I shall take that as a vote of confidence. Come, there is not much time until your friend will be moved. Once he is, there will be no way we can reach him," the Viceroy said and beckoned for the men to follow as he set off down the alleyway to his right, the agent not far behind him.

The four Englishmen exchanged quizzical glances before they fell into step behind the two Chinese men.

The pace that the Viceroy set was much faster than that of the agent, but he still kept to the shadows to avoid being seen by anyone that might be on the streets or looking out of their windows.

The Viceroy led the men through Canton until they arrived at the building that had once been his headquarters.

"Mr Cartwright is in there. He is being held in cells beneath the building. He has one guard; a man that has been torturing him. No one else is here. Once you have your friend, you will need to leave the city quickly. There are only a few hours left before Commander Lin will come to have him moved. When he discovers that his prisoner has escaped, you will need to be far from here," the Viceroy said.

"And where will you be?" the chief constable asked.

"I will be at home, so when the Commander comes knocking on my door, there can be no doubt that I was nowhere near his prisoner when they went missing," the Viceroy smiled.

"How will we find our way out of the city?" Callum asked.

"I will wait for you here. If the Commander arrives before you come out of the building, I will leave. You must be quick," the agent said sharply.

"Then we should hurry," the chief constable sighed.

The building being empty, save for the torturer and prisoner, made the task of the four men much easier. Though none of them trusted the Viceroy enough to believe he was telling them the truth.

As they entered the building, the four men split into two groups. The brigadier and chief constable descended into the bowels of the building to rescue Henry Cartwright whilst

Mr Taylor, and Mr St. Vincent searched the rest of the building to ensure that there was no one lying in wait.

Harry was not worried about being set upon by the people that normally worked in the building, but that there would be soldiers hiding somewhere close by.

He led the way through the ground floor rooms, but there was no one on sight. Callum stayed close behind his friend as the pair searched through the offices. There were desks full of papers, but as they were all in Chinese, neither man could read them.

"We should check the upper floor," Callum said after the pair were certain that no one was hiding on the ground floor.

The two picked up a handful of papers from the desks that looked to be important and made their way to the large staircase to the upper floor.

Knowing that Henry Cartwright was being held beneath the former offices of the Viceroy did not help George and the chief constable to find the stairs that led down to the cell.

The door to the stairwell was well hidden, but after

some searching, the two older men managed to find the stairway they were looking for.

George gripped the stick in his hand tightly as he followed Captain Jonnes Smith down into the depths of the building's foundations.

The chief constable moved quickly, he was excited, and the adrenaline was coursing through his veins as they reached the bottom of the stairs.

There was darkness all around the two men aside from light that was bleeding from around a doorway to their left.

The two men took a deep breath. George felt carefully for the handle on the door and pulled it open as quickly as he could. The chief constable rushed into the room, and his head met with something solid.

George was a few steps behind Captain Jonnes Smith and saw the torturer swing a metal poker at the chief constable's head.

The torturer was off-balance when George rushed him and knocked him to the ground. The stick he was holding went sliding across the floor, and the torturer dropped his metal poker.

The brigadier used his weight to pin the smaller man to the floor as the chief constable recovered himself.

"Go find Henry; I will deal with this," George ordered as the torturer struggled underneath him.

The chief constable nodded and went to search the three rooms that lay off the room that they had barrelled into.

The brigadier looked around the room now that the immediate danger was dealt with for the moment. There was a large bracer in the centre of the room that lit the room and had a large vat of water being heated over it.

The basin was large enough for a man to be placed inside of it and the thought of what the torturer was preparing to do with it made George sick to his stomach.

The small man was still struggling under the brigadier, but by the time the chief constable returned to the central room, the torturer was dead. His neck had been snapped, and he lay on the floor at the feet of the brigadier.

"Have you found him?" George asked as he stepped away from the corpse of the torturer.

"Yes, but I will need your help," the chief constable

said as he drew his eyes away from the torturer's body.

He didn't comment on the death of the man; in fact, he felt glad that the creature was dead and he was sure that George would feel glad for killing the torturer when he saw Henry.

The brigadier followed Captain Jonnes Smith into the small cell. The room was filled with a foul stench that was so overwhelming that it caused the seasoned soldier to recoil slightly as he entered.

The light in the room was dim as the only light being cast came from the brazier in the next room.

In the centre of the room, a small figure was tied on his knees. He was painfully thin, and parts of his flesh had been carved away. He was coughing and rasping and once would have been recognisable as Henry Cartwright, but now he was nothing more than a shaking mass.

George felt anger rising in his chest, seeing the former thief reduced to such a condition by the man who now lay dead in the next room.

"Henry? Can you hear me?" the brigadier asked gently as he cut the bonds that held Mr Cartwright's hands and feet together.

Henry couldn't reply and was in such bad condition that all he could do was fall forwards into the waiting arms of the chief constable.

"We should go," Captain Jonnes Smith said as he gently put one of Henry's arms around his neck and waited for George to do the same.

The two men carefully lifted their friend to his feet and slowly made their way out of the basement of nightmares.

"Are we waiting for the other two?" the chief constable grunted as they reached the top of the stairs and barged their way through the door to the lobby.

"No, we go now, it's their own fault if they stay too long and get left behind," the brigadier replied gruffly.

The two men made their way outside to meet with the agent, only to find that Harry and Callum were already there.

"Good, you're here. We have to go now," the agent said urgently.

The party of six men set off on the return journey to the warehouse. As slow as their progress had been on the

133

way there, it was even slower now.

It took almost an hour for the men to make their way back to the warehouse, by which point, Henry Cartwright was barely breathing.

"My God! What have they done to him?" Mr Marsh asked with horror when they finally staggered into the warehouse.

"I don't know, and the man who did it to him won't be able to do it to anyone ever again," the brigadier grunted as he and the chief constable lowered their injured friend to the ground.

"You cannot stay here, we must leave Canton. Commander Lin will be looking for this man everywhere. We must leave now," the agent urged.

"We have a Chinese Junk that is ready to take you through the blockade. It is going to be risky, but Mr Cartwright is in no condition to swim," Mr Smith said as he approached the group from the rear of the warehouse.

"How did you know his condition?" the chief constable frowned.

"He is not the first man to fall into the hands of

Commander Lin that I have seen. He is lucky to have friends that came to rescue him," Mr Smith replied in a sombre tone.

"The junk is ready?" Mr Taylor asked.

"It is, but you must stay below decks until the crew comes to fetch you," Mr Smith said.

"Where are they taking us?" Callum asked.

"To the hulks at Whampoa. They are armed, and Commander Lin will be unable to reach you there," Mr Smith replied.

"Then, we shall hurry. Thank you for your help," the chief constable said as Harry and Callum came forward to help Henry Cartwright out of the warehouse.

Mr Smith led the way from the warehouse to where the junk was waiting. There were no soldiers on the docks, which struck the chief constable as strange, but he was in such a hurry he did not have a moment to comment on it.

The men were herded quickly below deck and forced to sit in cramped conditions in the hull. They all knew it was safer for them to be hidden amongst the cargo, but it was not the best place for Henry Cartwright to be stuffed in his current condition.

The junk moved off from the dock, and Mr Smith melted into the shadows of the night. To begin with, there was nothing to cause the Englishmen any concern but as the junk sailed closer to the blockade the sound of raised voices and pounding feet on the deck above caused each of the men to hold their breath.

The shouting in Chinese grew louder, but the ship kept sailing. After a few minutes, the voices returned to normal, and the Englishmen knew that they were through the blockade and on their way to the hulks at Whampoa.

"How long do you think it will be before we can return to Calcutta?" Callum asked as he studied Henry's injuries.

"I don't know, but I hope it is soon," the brigadier replied with worry.

"The hulks are a safe place with plenty of food, water and warm beds. It will not matter if we are there for weeks or days," Harry shrugged.

"It will matter, any more than a few days and Henry may not live to see England again," the chief constable replied.

The four men lapsed into silence, and each man prayed they would not be hiding on the hulks for long.

Chapter 19

The hulks at Whampoa were full of activity as the junk drew alongside and the Englishmen and cargo were fetched from its belly.

"Why can't the British people in Canton escape in the belly of junks?" Callum asked as he disembarked and the doctor on the hulks pushed past him to go down to Henry Cartwright.

"There are too many of them, and it would not take long for the commander to discover how people are fleeing from the port," the man who managed the hulks said as he came to greet the new arrivals.

"You have a doctor here? I am impressed," the chief constable said as he was the next to step off the junk onto the hulks.

"We are here for long periods of time. Men get injured when they are working here. They get sick and fall overboard. It made good business sense to pay a doctor to live here too," the hulks manager shrugged, "The doctor will be some time examining your friend. The captain of the junk passed a message to me from Mr Smith. He told me everything that you have endured, and it seemed wise for the doctor to be called to check on Mr Cartwright. Come, we have beds and hot food waiting for,"

The four men followed the hulks manager as he led the way into one of the many cabins that lay in the network of boats that were anchored together.

They ate and found that exhaustion was overwhelming them after their night jaunt. It did not take long for them to crawl into their waiting cots and fall asleep.

When they awoke, the doctor had treated and bandaged each of the wounds on Henry Cartwright's body so that he looked more like a man than an injured beast.

But he was still unable to talk. All he could do was lie in the cot in the doctor's cabin.

"How is he, doctor?" the brigadier asked as he came to check on the former thief.

"Alive for now. He has more broken bones than I have seen in a long time and a rising fever that could yet kill him. You need to get back to dry land as soon as you can," the doctor replied.

"That is out of our hands, all we can do is wait," the brigadier sighed as he sat on a sea chest beside Henry's cot.

He spent the day waiting and talking to his old friend and only left to eat with the others. For three days the men were stranded on the hulks, and Henry's health continued to decline.

Every day, the brigadier went to sit with him whilst Captain Jonnes Smith went to look for signs of ships approaching on the horizon.

A few Chinese junks attempted to draw close to the hulks, their decks stuffed with soldiers on the Commander's orders, but cannons mounted to the hulks soon drove them away.

It took seven days for the ship sailing back to Calcutta dock at the hulks and another day before the Englishmen could board and the ship began its journey back to India.

When they arrived at the port of Calcutta, there was no carriage waiting for them. Harry and Callum went to find some suitable transportation to carry them to Lady de Mandeville's estate. Whilst they were gone, the brigadier and chief constable carried Henry from the boat on a litter.

They were waiting for several hours before Callum and Harry returned. By the time they reached Lady de Mandeville's estate, it was dark, but the household was not yet gone to bed.

"Send for the doctor," Carol-Ann ordered as she saw the men unloading the litter with the injured man on. She ushered them into the main house and into one of the large lounges on the ground floor of the house.

"And they call us barbarians," Sir Finlay muttered under his breath as Henry was carried into the house.

"Your grace, is my brother still here? We found these papers in the Commander's headquarters, but we need someone who can translate them," Callum asked as he fell into step beside his employer as they entered the house.

"He has gone to Malwa to oversee the growth of poppies and production of opium," Lady de Mandeville lied.

"Then these papers will have to be translated by someone else," Callum sighed.

"You should ask Superintendent Crump to read the letters. He can read several of the Chinese and Indian dialects. It is something that has proven extremely useful

141

over the years," Carol-Ann smiled warmly at Mr St. Vincent, something he had never seen before.

"What do we do now?" the brigadier asked.

"We wait for the doctor, once he has seen Mr Cartwright, we will call on Miss Baker to see what she has learned and then perhaps you will be able to go home. Mr Taylor and Mr St. Vincent will be going back to China, but where in China will depend on what Miss Baker has learned," Lady de Mandeville replied coldly.

It did not take long for the doctor to arrive at the estate, but his examination of Henry seemed to take hours. It was only a few minutes before midnight before he was able to give his professional opinion.

"How is he, doctor?" the chief constable asked as the doctor stood up from beside Mr Cartwright.

"Not at all well. I am afraid he is much too ill to travel. Even if he simply stays here to rest, I am not sure he will last more than a few days. His injuries are extensive, and some are beyond my ability to heal. His fate is in God's hands now," the doctor said sadly.

"Then he will have to stay here. I can ensure that he is

well cared for and made comfortable whilst he heals," Lady de Mandeville said calmly and the doctor nodded his agreement.

"Very well, though it would be appreciated if you could write to me about his condition," the countess said slowly.

"Then I shall endeavour to do so," the duchess replied with a wry smile.

Chapter 20

Lady de Mandeville was an excellent hostess, even to those that considered her an enemy. Brigadier George Webb-Kneelingroach could not fault the woman on her hospitality, though he refused to be anything other than civil to her. Countess Szonja had tried to speak to the brigadier in private several times since he had arrived at the house, but the worry over the consideration of Henry Cartwright and the flurry of activity that the arrival of the five men had caused had made it virtually impossible for her to talk to him alone.

The morning after their arrival, Lady de Mandeville had sent for Miss Baker, and the superintendent had come to read the papers that Harry and Callum had taken from the Commander's headquarters.

The brigadier had chosen to sit with Henry and watch as the doctor strictly instructed the servants as to how to care for the injured man. Henry had briefly opened his eyes, only to lapse back into an unconsciousness state almost immediately.

The countess had no desire to spend any longer

144

looking at the disfigured form of Mr Cartwright than she had to. Instead, she chose to sit in the rose garden under the shade of one of the giant trees that Lady Carol-Ann had ordered be placed in her garden to shield herself and her guests from the harsh Indian sun.

Sir Finlay had joined her in the rose garden momentarily after breakfast, but he was called away from the estate to deal with a legal matter.

Mr Dent had arrived not long after Sir Finlay had departed with some of the members of the Company board to discuss what had happened in Canton and how they should proceed with trade in China.

The chief constable spent the morning in the company of the superintendent discussing the finer points of British and India law enforcement whilst the superintendent attempted to translate the papers Lady de Mandeville had given to him.

Harry and Callum both spent their time riding the polo ponies that Lady de Mandeville stabled at the estate, enjoying themselves for the little time they had before they had to set off for China once more.

Miss Baker didn't arrive at the estate until after lunch and was so distressed at seeing Mr Cartwright so badly wounded that she fainted. It was almost time for the evening meal before she was able to relate everything that she had learned in her dressmaker's shop.

"The new opium trading posts in Chusan and the other ports to the north and east of Canton have been successfully established. The captains report that the shipments are going well and that within a year we – you shall be trading even more opium than before," Miss Baker informed Lady de Mandeville, Mr Dent and the members of the board that had been keenly awaiting new information.

"That is excellent news!" Mr Dent cried and felt a certain level of smug satisfaction at having beaten Commander Lin's attempts to end the opium trade after the merchant had been persecuted by the Imperial High Commissioner of Canton.

"Is there any news from England?" Mr Hogg asked on behalf of the other members of the board.

"Commander Lin's demands have been universally rejected, and there are rumours that Lord Palmerston intends

146

to pursue military action as soon as Parliament agrees to it. This letter was delivered to me ordering the recall of all agents to report on the situation here. Lord Palmerston expects us to report to him upon our return to England. There is also a rumour that he has told Governor Auckland to prepare for military forces to be deployed into China," Miss Baker continued.

"That news is even better. I will write to my husband if you would be kind enough to deliver the letter and inform him of how imperative military action in Canton is. That should help to get action approved quickly. At least quickly as far as Parliament is concerned," Lady de Mandeville smiled, and a chuckle of appreciation rippled around the room. It was clear to Miss Baker that none of those involved in trade believed that any government acted with anything close to speed.

"And in the meantime, we shall ignore Captain Elliot and continue trade operations outside of Canton," Mr Dent said, clapping his hands with glee.

"I will arrange for a boat to take you, the chief constable, the brigadier and the countess back to England as soon as possible," Lady de Mandeville assured the seamstress.

"But not Mr Cartwright, your grace?" Miss Baker asked with an edge of sadness to her voice.

"I am afraid not. Mr Cartwright is much too ill to be moved, and if he were to sail to England, it would be unlikely that he would reach Bombay alive. The journey is just too much for him. He will remain here where my servants can care for him, and the doctor shall attend him, maybe one day he will be able to see England again," Lady de Mandeville said gently.

"Then I must stay with him," Miss Baker said desperately.

"Angela, you have two sons to care for in England. You can do more for them than you can for Henry. Go home to them. Your friend will be safe and well-cared for here," the duchess said softly as she placed her gloved hand gently on the quivering hands of the seamstress.

Miss Baker was silent as she looked at the face of Lady de Mandeville. She was normally someone and guarded in her countenance, but in this moment there was tenderness and sincerity that caused Miss Baker to breakdown to tears and sobbingly agree to return to England.

Lady de Mandeville called for Samit to take Miss Baker to rest in her room until dinner was ready. As the crying woman was led from the room, the superintendent brought the translated letters for the duchess to read.

"What did they say?" Mr Dent asked with a frown as he watched Lady de Mandeville carefully reading through the letters and turning pages faced down on her desk.

"They are mostly unimportant reports but this letter you might find interesting," the duchess grinned.

"Oh?" Mr Dent asked as she handed him the letter.

"What does it say?" Mr Agnew of the East India Company asked with a mild edge of frustration to his voice.

"It says that the Emperor of China is very disappointed with Commander Lin. His destruction of the opium has done nothing to stop the drug finding its way into China," Mr Dent grinned.

"Then the emperor already knows of the new trade routes and Commander Lin's failure," Mr Hogg said with delight.

"The Viceroy will be pleased with this news. Though it will be interesting to see whether the plan outlined in this letter has any success," Lady de Mandeville said thoughtfully as she read the final piece of translations.

"And what plan is this?" Mr Dent asked.

"Commander Lin plans to open a clinic of sorts to help those addicted to opium to give up the drug," she replied.

"A noble goal indeed, but one I doubt that will gain any success. I cannot imagine that many people will go to such a place for fear of it being a trap and being sentenced to death by the Emperor for their addiction," Mr Agnew said with a snort.

"As long as it does not affect our business, it is none of our concern," Mr Hogg replied with a shrug.

The bell rang for dinner, ending the discussion about the Chinese situation and trade. Mr Dent and the gentlemen from the East India Company bid Lady de Mandeville good night, and she joined her guests for dinner.

Sir Finlay had not returned from the city, so there were only eight for dinner. The conversation during the meal was surprisingly light, though the duchess barely spoke a word. Instead, she listened contentedly to her guests and felt satisfied that she had done all that she could to secure British interests in China.

After the entrées had been cleared away, Samit came in with a letter for Lady de Mandeville.

"I'm sorry to interrupt your dining, but the messenger said that it was a matter of urgency," Samit apologised as the duchess opened the letter and slowly read it.

"I see, thank you, Samit, I believe that Mr St. Vincent will wish to read this," she said as she finished reading the message and handed the letter back to Samit for the head of the household to take round the table to where Callum sat.

Mr St. Vincent frowned as the letter was presented to him and he opened it with trembling hands,

Lord St. Vincent killed in rebel attack STOP Body returned to England STOP Lord died bravely in action STOP Report of skirmish to follow STOP Send obituary to Times once report read STOP.

Callum read the message and then let it fall to the floor.

"I am sorry for your loss," Lady de Mandeville said kindly as Callum asked to be excused.

The countess watched the duchess carefully for the rest of the meal. She knew that the telegram was a fabrication and that this lie was far kinder for the new lord to mourn than the truth. Yet she found it difficult to believe that Lady de Mandeville could so easily lie about murdering a man, even if he was a scoundrel and a traitor.

The rest of the meal passed in silence, no one feeling the need to talk. After dinner, the duchess left to arrange a vessel to carry the agents back to England. The chief constable and superintendent engaged themselves in a game of poorly played chess, and Miss Baker went to sit with Mr Cartwright whilst she could.

Mr Taylor went to check on the new Lord St. Vincent, and the countess finally had the opportunity to speak to the brigadier alone.

The pair retired to the veranda and the pleasant heat of the warm Indian evening.

"It will be a terrible shock to return to the cold of England," the brigadier chuckled.

"I imagine you would stay here longer if you could, you must have many happy years of your time here," the countess replied.

"I do indeed, but I have my son and ward awaiting my return to Grangeback, and I can hardly leave the dear children to fend for themselves," George replied with a sigh.

He was truly relieved to have survived his time in India and China and was resolved to never be dragged out on such a fool errand again.

"That is true, though there is something I need to tell you before we return to England," Szonja sighed.

"Oh? You have discovered something during your time here?" the brigadier asked with sudden interest.

"Yes, and I am sure that you will not want to hear all I have to say, but that cannot be helped," the countess replied and began to tell George about the papers, the murder of Lord Joshua St. Vincent, and the actions of Colonel Montgomery Baird.

Historical Note

Lord Francis Napier was born in 1758 and died in 1823. He was the 8th Lord Napier and served as an officer in the British Army and as a peer in the House of Lords. He served in Canada, fought with the Convention Army during the American Revolutionary War and escaped from captivity after the defeat and surrender at the Battle of Saratoga. He had five daughters and four sons and laid the foundation stone of the new buildings of the University of Edinburgh in 1789. He died at his home in 1823 when his son, William, inherited his title.

Lord William Napier was the 9th Lord Napier and did die in Macau whilst serving as the Chief Superintendent of British Trade in China in 1834. He was the first man to hold the office and only held it from 31st December 1833 to 11th October 1834, when he died. He was appointed to the position by Lord Palmerston, the Foreign Secretary of the time and the position was only created after the East India Company's monopoly of trade in the Far East was ended.

The occupation of Hong Kong, which you shall read about in a moment, was originally Lord William Napier's idea. It was mentioned in a dispatch to Lord Palmerston dated 14th August 1834 in which he suggested a commercial treaty, backed by a small armed force should be attempted to secure European trading rights in China. He recommended that a British force of small size "should take possession of the Island of Hongkong, in the eastern entrance of the Canton River, which is admirably adapted for every purpose."

He was originally buried in Macau after his death, but his body was later exhumed and sent home to be reburied at Ettrick in Scotland. He was married to Elizabeth Cochrane-Johnstone and had two sons and six daughters. His eldest son, Francis, became the 10th Lord Napier upon William's death.

Each member of the board of the East India Company I mention by name was a director of the board of the East India Company around the time each part of the book is set. I have taken some creative leaps with how the board of the

Company operated and how they interacted with Lady de Mandeville, but as far as their names go – they are accurate.

Opium as a way to balance the silver the East India Company was spending on silk and tea presented itself as a solution in 1767 as the consumption of the drug was rising and it was first proposed by Mr Watson at a meeting in Calcutta. However, until 1794 the opium runs were largely unsuccessful – unlike the Portuguese opium dealing.

The change in how the British were attempting to deal with the Chinese changed in 1794 when Lord George Macartney's diplomatic mission to China failed. He had gone in 1793 to secure a formal trade agreement with Emperor Ch'ien-lung. Macartney had been sent by King George III to secure equal representation, free trade, a British trading port and a permanent embassy in the Chinese capital. Up until this point, the British wanted to sell their Indian cotton to the Chinese and purchase their tea and silk. Opium wasn't a major issue at this point, and the East India Company was even willing to forbid the exportation of its Indian opium into China if the Emperor would grant the port, embassy, and equal and free trade agreement.

Instead of agreeing to this, Emperor Ch'ien-lung sent Macartney back to King George III with a letter. There would be no commissioner or embassy in Peking. There was already a trading port at Canton that the British must use and all trade had to go through the hong merchants. China was a Celestial Empire and saw every other nation as beneath it so there could be no equal trading. The Emperor believed the idea of striking a trade agreement with the British with the conditions proposed to be an evil example that would be followed by other European nations. He added that he was not offended by the barbarian king George. "I do not forget the lonely remoteness of your island, cut off from the world by intervening wastes of sea, nor do I overlook your excusable ignorance of the usages of our Celestial Empire." He also warned King George III not to attempt to trade anywhere in China outside of Canton and Macau and that there would be no reduction on trade tariffs, "Do not say you were not warned in due time! Tremblingly obey and show no negligence!"

As there was to be no trade agreement and no reason to restrict the sale of opium, a hulk sailed for Whampoa in 1794 and spent a year trading opium off the coast of China – something that proved very profitable to them. Just how profitable I will come to in a moment.

The family of Lady de Mandeville are all fictional, so there was no ruination and expulsion of a Lord to India that the Egerton family played a part in. The political record of the Egertons is, however, against the East India Company holding a trade monopoly.

The East India Company still exists and thrives today, though the days of growing opium in India and smuggling it into China are long gone. There was no British policy on the importing and growing of opium at the time, which made Captain Elliot's task of maintaining trade relations especially difficult.

The production of opium is a rather long process. It had been grown in India for a long time before the start of the Opium Wars, but it was the East India Company that turned it into an immense and highly profitable industry. No poppies could be grown in the provinces of India, Bihar and Benares without the expressed permission of the Company. No opium could leave India without passing through the hands of the Company either.

Landowners in India and the Company turned over increasing amounts of land to growing opium, and it was the best land that had to be used. The Papaver somniferum is not the hardiest of flowers and requires rich soil and constant irrigation to grow. More money could be made from growing opium than growing grain, however.

The land was ploughed three times, then weeded, and then scored with channels for irrigation. The poppy seeds were sown in November, and by March the flowers had dropped their petals and were ready to be harvested. The pods on the poppies had knife slits made in the sides that allowed the poppy juice to leak out. This was hardened by the sun and scraped off. These scrapings were then delivered to village officers. Each farmer could only produce an ounce a day. The process was a tedious and long one, but it was something that the farmers had to undertake.

If a farmer refused to grow opium, then the agents of the East India Company in Benares and Bihar could capitalise the farmer (throw a handful of coins into his home and then place him under house arrest) until he submitted and agreed to grow what the Company wanted.

A sharecropper would also tour the poppy fields of each farmer and roughly estimate how much opium they should produce each year based on the number of flowers that were growing. The estimate given was the minimum that a farm should produce and a price was agreed for the crop during these tours. If the farmer failed to achieve the minimum yield, he could be sued for embezzlement.

This stopped farmers and their workers from keeping the

opium and even smoking the product that they farmed – something the East India Company was very keen to restrict in India, except for medicinal usage.

Once the village officers had the raw opium, it was delivered to the Company depots for processing. During this process, it was pressed into cakes that are roughly the size of a clenched fist and them wrapped in dry poppy leaves to create a crust. After this, they were packed into mango-wood chests that contain between 125 and 140 pounds of opium as there was no standard weight for the product. One chest of opium could supply 8,000 opium addicts, with the worst addiction, with enough of the drug to last them a month.

We still have a problem with opium addiction today in the form of morphine and heroin addiction. When opium is refined, you get morphine, when morphine is refined further, you get heroin. There are different types of heroin that are created through different processes of refinement.

Those reading the history of Opium Wars and the actions of

161

the Chinese to stem the tide of the smuggling may notice many parallels with the modern war on drugs and the same ineffective methods being used. Though the penalties for drug use are nowhere near as extreme as those in the Celestial Empire, history does repeat itself and only by studying and learning from history can we move forward and not repeat the same mistakes – we may make new ones, but that is a completely separate issue.

It was through military intervention in 1840 that the notion of gunboat diplomacy came into existence. Lord Palmerston sent a letter to Elliot in November 1839, but the matter wasn't debated in Parliament until 1840 when gunboats were dispatched. You may now understand why Lady de Mandeville, Mr Dent and the members of the East India Company board found speed on the part of Parliament to be so amusing.

The causes of the Opium War are not merely rooted in the trade of opium, as the name suggests. The trade of opium was a point of contention, but it was the attitude of the

Chinese through decades of attempts to trade with them and the high-handed manner that Commander Lin dealt with the opium situation in Canton that prompted the use of military action.

The exile of William Jardine and the persecution of Lancelot Dent both happened. The Viceroy may have been as I have portrayed him, but I find it somewhat unlikely. He was guilty of accepting bribes and did attempt to deceive Emperor Ch'ien-lung over his complicity in the trade.

Commander Lin Tse-hsü was appointed as the Imperial High Commissioner and arrived in Canton in March 1839 to take the barbarians in hand and bring an end to the trade. Captain Elliot was not a popular man amongst the merchants or East India Company when he tried to pacify Commander Lin, and he did hand over the 20,283 chests of opium into Chinese hands – which you will now understand is a rather more considerable amount of opium than you might have first assumed.

Captain Elliot's issuing of a promissory note to the merchants that had their opium handed over to Commander Lin were not lucky enough to have it endorsed immediately. The notes were a point of contention between the government and the merchants, and it was years until the matter was settled – which if you consider how much money each chest was worth, is a very long time for even rich merchants to be out of pocket; though it is understandable that the government would not have wanted to pay out so much money to the merchants when they had no opium policy and Captain Elliot had acted without a mandate.

Despite the lack of a policy, smuggling ships filled with opium sailed under British colours and were afforded the protection of the British Navy as the skirmishes fought with the Chinese prior to the full naval deployment in response to the oppressive actions of Commander Lin.

The edicts that Commander Lin were exactly as I have described and he did spend months destroying the opium chests he seized and pouring them into the river. The British people in Canton were under siege, though I have no evidence that any were ever captured and tortured in the manner that Henry Cartwright was. Ultimately though, Commander Lin did fail in ending the opium trade in China. In May 1840, he did set up a clinic to treat opium addicts outside of Canton, but very few people went for treatment, and the death penalty did nothing to stop the addicts.

Lord Palmerston agreed with the opinion that Commander Lin had gone too far and that military action was justified to bring an end to the oppression in Canton.

The first action of the Opium War was fought on 4th September 1839. It was a minor skirmish between British and Chinese ships in the Canton estuary and has become known as the Battle of Kowloon. The Chinese claimed it as a resounding victory, but really, nobody won it, and hardly anyone was hurt.

On 3rd November there was another sea battle between two British frigates – *Volage* and *Hyacinth* carrying refugees from

Canton – were attacked by a fleet of war junks. Both the British and Chinese claim to have won the battle, but around twelve of the junks were sunk, and the rest were sent running by the two British ships, so it is more likely to be considered a British victory.

This was just a small taste of what would happen when the British expeditionary force arrived on 21st June 1840. The Chinese had never faced an enemy like the British before, and the attitude that the barbarians were so inferior to them left the Chinese woefully unprepared for what would happen.

"One need only 'display the celestial terror', and the barbarians would run. If they ran, one advisor told the Emperor, they would trip; and everyone knew that the soldiers of this 'insignificant and detestable race,' weakened by 'the ravages of our climate,' were so tightly buttoned in their quaint uniforms that once down, they could never get up."

The lack of knowledge of European warfare was even more evident in the idea that the British musket was a sign of weakness, that they had no regard for ritual or precedent and no army could function without it.

The Chinese also faced problems with their marines constantly being seasick and the gunners of the defence batteries being corrupt. They were so corrupt that they had sold most of their gunpowder to British smugglers. This meant that they used sand mixed with gunpowder to try and fire their canons. One battery that overlooked the Canton estuary was using a mixture of 30% gunpowder and 70% sand in order to operate their guns.

Commander Lin reported that the Chinese marines got 1% of their pay from the Empire of China and the rest from the opium smugglers. Thus he blamed them for being unable to defeat the British.

The expeditionary force the British sent contained 16 warships carrying 4,000 troops. This was where gunboat diplomacy as a concept originated. They did not attack Canton but simply stayed off-shore for a few days before sailing north to the port of Ting-hai on Chusan island. The people of Ting-hair had no idea what was happening. They believed that they were smugglers come to trade and bring their wealth from Canton to their port. They effectively rolled out the red carpet, and 9 minutes later, after being bombarded by the broadsides of 15 ships, the port was almost nothing but rubble. The British troops then landed and swept through what remained of the port and outlying farms, looting raping and foraging - as it was recorded by one of the British diarists of the time "in a thousand instances received great injustice at our hands."

Chusan was occupied by the British, but the battles of the Opium Wars were sporadic and were small engagements that had no real planning. The British had wanted Chusan as their trading point since the late 1700s and the Emperor of China began to communicate with the barbarians. A letter from Lord Palmerston was given to the Emperor on 20th August 1840 in which Palmerston made 5 main demands:

1) The Chinese must communicate with the British Officials as equals.

2) The Chinese Government must pay the Cantonese guild-merchant's debt to the British traders.

3) The Chinese had to pay for the opium that was seized by Commander Lin.

4) The British war costs had to be reimbursed.

5) A "sufficiently large and properly situated island" must be given to the Crown as a permanent possession.

The Emperor refused. On 13th October, Commander Lin was stripped of his rank and brought to Peking for trial. He had failed to stop the opium trade and had brought the barbarian fleet down upon the Empire of China. Another official was named to replace him, but there was no stopping the British.

"On 7th January, 1841, the English fleet struck at the main defences of the Canton estuary, the forts at Taikok and Shakok. These fell: within 24 hours most of the Chinese fleet had been annihilated, and the War God's descendant,

Admiral Kuan, had asked for a truce."

The Chinese had been completely humiliated, and Canton was now at the mercy of the British forces. Ch'i-shan, the new Imperial High Commissioner, began to negotiate with Captain Elliot to try and save the people of Canton. He received a secret message from the Emperor to cease negotiating as 4,000 imperial troops were marching to Canton and would easily defeat the British. Ch'i-shan had an impossible choice to make – ignore the Emperor, commit treason and save Canton, or do as the Emperor commanded and lose Canton to the British.

He chose to keep negotiating. On 18th January 1841, Ch'i-shan gave Elliot a signed agreement that gave the British Hong Kong harbour and island. He then gave a banquet for the British where the details of the agreement were formalised. When the Emperor discovered what had happened, he condemned Ch'i-shan to death and had him brought to Peking in chains. His fortune and land were seized for the Emperor, but Ch'i-shan was allowed to live in exile, just as

Commander Lin had been.

The Emperor sent more men to Canton to try and defeat the barbarians, but they could not be stopped. On 21st May the last of the Canton defences had been destroyed. The British were given £600,000 to leave Canton and spare the city. Captain Elliot was content with this figure, but Lord Palmerston, the Prime Minister and the Company directors were not happy. Hong Kong was a barren island, and the £600,000 did not come close to covering the expenses that Palmerston had demanded compensation for. Elliot was then sacked for ignoring Palmerston's instructions.

This was not the end of the Opium Wars or the bloodshed. At Ningpo, the British took the city, and the Chinese planned a counterattack. They planned it to take place on the Day of the Tiger (10th March) at the Hour of the Tiger (between 15:00 and 17:00) and made no secret of this. When they opened the gates to rush the barbarians, the Chinese were cut down by the strategically laid mine-field outside the city. It was a military disaster for the Chinese. The British spent the winter in Ningpo and then moved on towards Peking.

Shanghai fell to the British in June, and in August the British sailed to Nanking. On 29th August the Treaty of Nanking was signed, and the Opium War was over. The Chinese had nothing left to bargain with, and so the British wrote their own treaty. The Chinese ended up paying over £2,000,000 in compensation to the British. Canton was opened to foreign trade, though it was mostly British, and there were four new treaty ports – Shanghai, Ningpo, Foochow and Amoy. All of these places were unrestricted to the British, and they were treated as equals there, not barbarians. Hong Kong officially became the property of the Crown and was transformed by the British into the Gibraltar of the Far East (though there aren't as many monkeys in Hong Kong – if you haven't been to Gibraltar, there are a lot of monkeys there).

Finally, the Chinese had no power to stop the trade of opium, and Chinese consumption soared from 2,000 tons a year in 1843 to almost 5,000 by 1866.

Because of the Opium War, Britain became the master of the

Far East, but it was the end of the Chinese Empire. The last Empire of the ancient world, which had stood for 4,000 years, had fallen to the barbarians. The collapse of Imperial China began, and Communist China rose. Something that may not have happened if Commander Lin had not been so heavy-handed or the British had not taken the affront so badly and responded with military action. There were faults and injustices on both sides of the Opium Wars, the British were not the villains that they are often portrayed as and the Chinese were not innocent victims of colonialisation.

The Japanese, however, learned the lessons of gunboat diplomacy and pre-emptive action better than the Chinese and it has been argued that the Opium Wars were the first psychological push to the Japanese on their road to Pearl Harbour.

Mr Marsh and Mr Smith are complete fiction; there may well have been a Mr Smith and Mr Marsh working in Canton at the time of the Opium Wars, but these individuals were both my own plot devices and nothing more. There was also no ban on sailing at the start of the Opium Wars; I merely had to find a reason that the kidnappers of Grace and Millie could not escape the country with the girls at the end of *A Bonfire Surprise in Stickleback Hollow*.

This book deals with the trade aspect and war that drug use was a major issue in, but it does not deal with the side of addiction and the damage that it **can** cause both, physically and emotionally. Though I do believe in freedom of choice, if you know anyone that is addicted to drugs (both legal and illegal) and wants help or you want to learn more about drugs, the dangers effects and ways to get treatment then there are several free places that you can go to for advice. In the UK there is FRANK where you can find all sorts of information and help for free – www.talktofrank.com. Mind, the mental health charity in the UK also offer support and advice about drug addiction – www.mind.org.uk. There are also sites such as www.drugwise.org.uk and www.urban75.com where you can find help and advice. These are all services that operate in the UK, however, for those in the USA https://drugfree.org has advice and information that you may find useful. If none of these sites are of help to you, a quick google search of "free drug advice" should provide you with local options that are relevant to you. There are also specific charities and support groups that are set up to help individuals with specific additions from alcohol to painkillers and crystal meth to LSD.

Like this book? Need to know what happens next?

Click here: https://mybook.to/BerryPickers to get The March of the Berry Pickers, book 8 in the Mysteries of Stickleback Hollow series.

Love this book so much you want the rest of the series? You can get it by clicking here: http://mybook.to/sticklebackhollow to go to the series page and buy them all on Kindle with one click.

Thanks so much for taking the time to read my book. I hope you enjoyed it. If you did, and you would like to leave a review, you can do so here: https://mybook.to/henrycartwright.

You can also sign up for my newsletter here: http://eepurl.com/g_sVRP to stay up-to-date with all my latest news and new releases.

Like this book? Need to know what happens next.

Click here _____ to get The March of the Berry Pickers, book 8 in the Mysteries of Stickleback Hollow series.

Love this book so much you want the rest of the series? You can get it by clicking here:
_____ to go to the series page and buy them all on Kindle with one click.

Thanks so much for taking the time to read my book. I hope you enjoyed it. If you did and you would like to leave a review, you can do so here:
_____

You can also sign up for my newsletter here:
_____ to stay up-to-date with all my latest news and new releases.

<u>Also by the same author</u>

180

<u>Poetry</u>

Standing by the Watchtower: Volume 1
Standing by the Watchtower: Volume 2
Indie Visible: Vol. 1

<u>Shakespeare Simplified</u>
The Merchant of Venice
The Merchant of Venice Key Stage 3 Workbook
The Merchant of Venice Key Stage 3 Teacher's Guide

Further information on these titles can be found at
<u>www.mightierthanthesworduk.com</u>

Books Adapted by C.S. Woolley for Foxton Books

Level 1 400 Headwords

The Wizard of Oz by L. Frank Baum

The Adventures of Huckleberry Finn by Mark Twain

The Adventure of the Speckled Band by Arthur Conan Doyle

Anne of Green Gables by L. Maud Montgomery

Dracula by Bram Stoker

The Prisoner of Zenda by Anthony Hope

The Lost World by Arthur Conan Doyle

The Little Prince by Antonie de Saint-Exupéry

A Little Princess by Frances Hodges Burnett

The Secret Garden by Frances Hodges Burnett

Level 2 600 Headwords

Moby Dick by Herman Melville

Gulliver's Travels by Jonathan Swift

Alice in Wonderland by Lewis Carroll

Sleepy Hollow by Washington Irving

Treasure Island by Robert Louis Stevenson

Around the World in Eighty Days by Jules Verne

Robinson Crusoe by Daniel Defoe

Beauty and the Beast by Gabrielle-Suzanne Barbot de Villeneuve

Heidi by Johanna Spyri

The Jungle Book by Rudyard Kipling

Level 3 900 Headwords

The Three Musketeers by Alexandre Dumas

Pocahontas by Charles Dudley Warner

Oliver Twist by Charles Dickens

Frankenstein by Mary Shelly

Journey to the Centre of the Earth by Jules Verne

Call of the Wild by Jack London

Level 4 1300 Headwords

The Count of Monte Cristo by Alexandre Dumas

The Merchant of Venice by William Shakespeare

The Railway Children by Edith Nesbit

Jane Eyre by Charlotte Bronte

Level 5 1700 Headwords

The Thirty-Nine Steps by John Buchan

David Copperfield by Charles Dickens

Great Expectations by Charles Dickens

Twenty Thousand Leagues Under the Sea by Jules Verne

Level 6 2300 Headwords

Kidnapped by Robert Louis Stevenson

The Mysterious Island by Jules Verne

Other

11 Plus Flash Cards

For more information visit

http://www.foxtonbooks.co.uk

CPSIA information can be obtained
at www.ICGtesting.com
Printed in the USA
LVHW03070815102]
700519LV00007B/365